AURAS OF DECEIT

A Trivolity Cozy Mystery

AURAS OF DECEIT
A Trivolity Cozy Mystery

Annette Larkin

James W Salkeld

John Stickney

Sandra Warren

E Jax Willoughby

QSynQ Publishing
QSynQ.pub

DEDICATION

To our friends and families

and cozy mystery lovers everywhere.

ACKNOWLEDGMENTS

The authors wish to thank the following people:

Tom Williams for plot and character contributions

Cheri DeLaVergne for the cover artwork

Kay Hodgson and Pete Belz for insights and consultation

Table of Contents

The Party

"I can't believe I agreed to that stupid game," Naomi muttered, while yanking hangers right and left along the rod in her closet, looking for just the right dress. Gunther, as usual, would expect her to outshine every other woman attending the party. She was getting tired of being his 'arm candy'. Soon, neighbors in her new Trivolity community would know the truth of their relationship anyway, so why put on airs? Frowning, she uncovered a midnight blue sheath from the protective cover and slipped it on.

Realizing a diamond choker was a bit much for the ridiculous Murder Mystery themed party, she considered selecting something else. However, the choker contrasted nicely with the dress and even seemed to make her chocolate-colored irises a shade of purple; yes, Elizabeth Taylor all the way. Of course, it could be the chandelier lighting.

1

Gunther had initially protested when she insisted on finishing the loft rooms as her She-Cave with tri-fold full-length mirrors and a Baccarat Museum Chandelier. Her purring persuasions succeeded when she pointed out that Gunther's own extensive wardrobe would fill most of the upgraded master bedroom closet. He certainly did not want to wrinkle those hand-tailored suits by over-packing the closet rods, did he? He did not!

"Gunther!" Naomi called down from her She-Cave dressing room, "Gunther, I need you to zip me up!"

"Be right there!" Gunther took the stairs to Naomi's loft bedroom, two at a time. He gasped when he saw her, and wondered how he could even think of giving her up? If only her warmth equaled her beauty. Smiling, he said, "You look stunning, my dear."

"Oh gawd," Naomi muttered through her exaggerated toothy smile. There stood Galant Gunther in his gray tuxedo, looking like a butler.

Naomi abruptly spun around to keep from laughing, glad to have chosen to wear the over-the-top choker. With one sweep of her hair, she moved her long sable tresses clear of the zipper.

"Thanks," she said when he finished, then turned to face him, eyes narrowed. "So, tell me again about this game. Murder, you called it?"

"It's not as ominous as it sounds. It'll be fun and get folks talking to each other!"

"Well, explain it to me again," Naomi said. "Didn't you say people will be walking all through the house?"

Gunther gave a charming smile. "It'll be fine. Our guests will each pull a piece of paper out of the bowl. All will be blank except for two: one will say Investigator and the other will say Murderer. The murderer kills by tweaking someone's elbow. That person falls to the floor. Whoever finds a body yells, 'There's a body in here!' after which everyone freezes. The Investigator comes running, surveys the scene, and then directs everyone to gather in the great room for the interrogation. It's that simple."

Naomi glared at Gunther. "You left out the part where they'll be walking through the house from room to room with the lights out. Really, Gunther. With the lights out?"

"Well, they must move around so the Murderer can choose a victim. Please, dearest, you need not worry yourself. Simply lock your door if you don't want anyone to go into your She-Cave."

"Very funny! You know there's no lock on my door! This is a harebrained idea, Gunther. I don't like it! I don't like it at all!"

Just then, the doorbell chimed.

"Shit!" Naomi fled into her bathroom. "I haven't

finished my makeup!"

Gunther ran downstairs, checked himself in the hall mirror, put on his most charming smile, and opened the door. When he saw who it was, he double-checked to make sure Naomi was out of sight and wrapped Bethann in a very long hug. When she pulled away, he planted one on her lips.

"What're you doing?" Bethann whispered. "Someone might see!"

"Naomi's upstairs out of earshot, and you're the first to arrive," Gunther whispered back, leaning forward to make sure no neighbors were approaching.

"Who is it?" came a voice from afar.

"If that's Bethann, send her up. And call the HOA again. I want that racket stopped before everyone gets here. If anyone goes out on the patio, they won't be able to hear themselves think with all that noise!"

Gunther hung his head and yelled sarcastically, "They're *tree frogs,* Naomi. The HOA can do nothing about *tree frogs*!"

"Well, what the hell do we pay them for? God!" Naomi said. "Just send Bethann up!"

Bethann gave Gunther an evil eye as she moved through the foyer and mouthed, "Out of earshot, huh?"

"Coming," Bethann yelled as she reached the stairs

and headed up to the loft. "Always the early bird! What can I do to help?"

"I'm so glad you came before the others," whispered Naomi, pulling Bethann into her bathroom. She paced back and forth in front of her enormous open shower. It was so big, four or more could shower at the same time. "Gunther's going to play this ridiculous Murder Game," she said. "He thinks access to the entire house will be fine, but I'm putting my foot down with the closets and bathrooms. I mean, can you imagine virtual strangers going in and out of those rooms? I don't want anyone in my bathroom. Do you understand?"

"Calm down, Naomi," Bethann said. "It won't be that bad. First of all, the guests are your neighbors, not virtual strangers. Secondly, I can help. Tell me what you want kept private and I'll make sure it happens."

"Oh, would you?" Naomi gushed. "You're a lifesaver!" With barely a breath in between, she pointed toward the stairs. "Would you mind checking up on the caterers? They were a last minute choice and I've always been suspicious of misspelled companies. Kookie's Kitchen Katering! Can you believe that name? It's too late now. Thanks! I need to finish my makeup!"

Bethann backed out of the bathroom and headed toward the stairs. The aromas of shrimp cocktail, pumpkin spice canapes and orange scones danced up the staircase as she descended. The array of delicious hors d'oeuvres was extensive. The only things amiss were the napkins and plates. One of the helpers put them at the wrong end of the custom marble top buffet. Bethann quickly corrected the error herself and then moved into the foyer where several other couples were gathered.

After politely acknowledging each group, Bethann cozied up to a potted plant in the foyer, but not before Troy spotted her. His eyes narrowed to sinister slits, almost foxlike. He stomped past her and growled.

Meanwhile, couples who had already arrived were grumbling about Gunther's tuxedo, since the invitation clearly stated, casual attire. Wait until they see Naomi, Bethann smirked. She had learned, shortly after the von Hapsburgs moved in, that nothing they do is *casual.*

From her vantage point, Bethann could see the stairway to Naomi's loft and the front door where neighbors kept arriving. The Buckets had just entered; Rusty wearing Dockers and a short-sleeved, navy blue shirt with little sailboats stitched into it, and Kitty in a sundress and carrying an oversized woven bag. Obviously, they believed the invitation. Bethann bit her lip, thinking about how Naomi would enjoy dishing about their fashions later. But wait! Oh my God! No! Kitty didn't really? Did she?

She brought her damn dog? Whoa! Wait until Naomi sees it. She hates that ratty animal. Sparks are going to fly. This party is getting more and more interesting by the minute. Bethann choked back a small giggle and raised her chin.

Suddenly, Bethann realized all conversation had stopped and all eyes had turned toward the stairway. And, like the grand lady Naomi thought she was, she came, slowly, step by step, down the stairs. She was beautiful, Bethann had to admit, and the dress she was wearing fit her like a glove; the color a perfect match to enhance her incredible eyes. But the condescending smile on her face was enough to turn the least discerning in the room against her. What the hell, Bethann thought. Why would Naomi and Gunther put on such a party if they felt that way? What's with the von Hapsburgs?

"Good evening, everyone! It's so nice of you to come!" Naomi stopped at the bottom rung, still elevated above her guests. "Gunther has planned a fun game for everyone to enjoy, so please, move into the great room so he can get started."

"Yes," echoed Gunther, leading folks from the foyer. "Go ahead and visit the open bar and then let the game begin!"

An Unfortunate Incident

Ed watched from the office window of his house across the street as the guests arrived at the von Hapsburgs. Most people traveled to the large home on foot or parked their golf carts along the curb. The retired detective concentrated on fitting in more pieces to the jigsaw puzzle, a pleasant Sonoran sunset, made from a picture he had taken himself years ago. It passed the time and was almost a kind of meditation.

Taking a sip of his scotch, he enjoyed the quiet, the bit of solitude, as his wife, Gina, had gone to the theater with the Going Solo club. Well, mostly quiet, except for the music emanating from the party across the street. His friend Bethann was offended on his behalf that he hadn't been invited.

Ed chuckled, remembering her indignant whine. "Really, how rude of them!" He didn't mind; the less he had to do with others, the better. Gina wasn't pleased with Bethann always trying to coax her husband out of the house. Like other wives, she looked at Bethann's attentions with suspicion. Likely with good cause, he thought.

Ed noticed Bethann had arrived at the party just after the caterers, no doubt to help Naomi out. This is just like a stakeout from the old days, he mused, only with scotch, not coffee. For old times' sake, he kept a log of the arrivals. He continued to work on the puzzle, as more guests arrived. He recognized Troy and the Buckets–Rusty and Kitty. "Interesting," Ed said out loud, noticing Troy rudely stepping in front of Kitty to enter the house.

He could swear he heard a dog barking, a small rat-sized kind of bark. Probably Xena smuggled in Kitty's purse. Ed smiled as he thought of Naomi's reaction when she discovered a dog at her party. Good for you, Kitty.

A man shambled up the street toward the party house. His clothing and unkempt appearance marked him as what some might call unique or eccentric. Ed marveled that Naomi and Gunther would even acknowledge such a person, let alone issue an invitation. His bewilderment resolved when the resident paused only briefly on the sidewalk, then continued up the street.

Returning to the puzzle, he reflected on how much he

enjoyed them. It was easy to see how the pieces fit together. Not like people. They never behaved the way they ought to. Ed always used to think the best of people. But he had been let down too many times; the last time just before retiring. He kept to himself now, mostly. That way, he wouldn't be disappointed.

Gina still had that optimism about people. Ed didn't want to take that away from her. When they had moved into their resale home at Trivolity, Gina had resolved to visit the neighbors, introducing themselves. "That's what you do," she had told him. He went along, hoping against hope for the best. Naomi von Hapsburg had taken one look at them and their small house, and that was that. It didn't help that Ed was a retired cop, and Gina had been a nurse. Naomi had left the impression that they were not the 'right people'.

Despite the von Hapsburgs' unfriendly attitude, he and Gina had made other friends in the community, like Troy and the Buckets and Bethann, although he wasn't so sure about her. Ed swirled the ice in his glass. He liked her, and their conversations were always friendly, but there seemed to be an undercurrent of unease surrounding Bethann. Gina had found plenty of social activities like line dancing, wine clubs, no, he corrected himself, not wine, rather book clubs. And he had his puzzles.

He was about to add a new piece to the scene when something across the street caught his eye.

"What the hell?" he muttered. "All the lights at the von Hapsburgs are out!" His power was still on, so it couldn't be an outage. "What on earth are they doing?" he mused. "Ah, well, to each their own." Ed returned to the puzzle, putting the piece in place.

Suddenly, his phone buzzed. It can't be Gina, he thought. She already texted a picture from the theater. He picked up his phone and opened the text. It was from Bethann:

"Help! I can't brea..."

Ed peered across the street again. He shrugged. Bethann and her games. She's probably bored already.

"Very funny!" he texted back.

He worked on a few more puzzle pieces, waiting for a response. They were getting harder to fit. "Damn it, Bethann! You've ruined my concentration." I won't be able to focus until I tell her off. He finished his scotch and headed across the street.

The front door was open, so Ed let himself in. The great room was packed with guests wandering around by candlelight. Caterers cautiously served trays of drinks and hors d'oeuvres. Bethann was nowhere to be seen, but he might have missed her in the dark. Finally, Ed spotted

Troy grabbing the arm of a passing waiter, nearly tipping the serving tray as he snagged a drink.

"Hey Troy!"

"Oh, hi Ed. I thought you hated parties like this," Troy replied, his voice rumbling deep.

"Yes, well. Bethann sent me a weird text. Have you seen her?"

"She's around here somewhere," Troy said.

Suddenly, a blood-curdling scream reverberated through the house from the direction of the foyer, followed by a shout, "There's a body in here!"

Everyone around them froze. Rusty shot past, heading for the stairway.

Ed started to follow when Troy grabbed his arm. "It's just a game," he said. "A murder mystery. Gunther's bright idea!"

"Ahh, that explains the text she sent. 'I can't breathe...' or something like that."

"Sounds like Bethann. Always dramatic!" Troy winked. "Probably a good thing we have an ex-cop here."

All around them, folks were returning to the great room. Troy turned to Ed. "Have something to eat while I go find the victim. Wait for my yell. Hey, Rusty! Get your butt over here and keep Ed company while I go do my bit. I'll be back soon."

"Why is Troy the only one concerned about the victim?" Ed asked as the other man sidled up.

"He must be the investigator in the game," Rusty explained. "The investigator has to check the scene and interview prospective murderers."

Troy headed up the stairs as Naomi came into the foyer. Realizing she had an uninvited guest, she narrowed her eyes and scanned Ed up and down. The glare she sent could have killed him right there. Damn, he thought. I should have changed out of my shorts and T-shirt before coming over; at least I wore sandals, he chuckled to himself. Gina won't be happy either when she finds out that: one, I crashed the von Hapsburg's party; two, I didn't put on decent clothes; and three, I went without her!

Rusty, feeling Naomi's wrath, whispered to Ed, "Don't worry. I'll keep you safe from the dragon lady."

"Thanks! Hey, where's his nibs? I should at least get a dressing down from both von Hapsburgs."

"Oh, somewhere around. Usually not far from Bethann, if you catch my drift. Hey, you're in the pickleball club, right? Do you have some cash on you for the dues? Since I've got you here."

"Rusty," Ed replied. "For the umpteenth time, I am not in—"

"My God!" He heard Troy yelling from upstairs. "It's

13

Bethann! She's dead!"

"Sorry, that's my cue. I'll get the money later. Everybody freeze!" yelled Rusty. "Close that door, nobody leaves!"

"Hey, that was good, Rusty," said Ed.

Troy came stumbling down the stairs. "Someone call 911!"

"Now, you don't need to get carried away, Troy," Gunther admonished, appearing from another room. "Let's just say I called 911 and we can get on with the game."

Troy was breathless. Ed noticed a familiar look of shock on the man's face. Clearly, Troy had seen something horrible. He went over and grabbed him by the shoulders. "It's true, isn't it? Not a game? She's really dead?"

Troy collapsed on the bottom stair. "Yes, dear God. She's... I think she's dead. She's in the bathroom."

"Rusty, call 911! And no one leaves! I'm going up!" Ed yelled.

Ed took the stairs two at a time, then gave in to his age and weight. Finally, he reached the top, gasping for breath. Gina's right, he thought. I need to start walking, at least. He surveyed the loft and waited for his breathing to get back to normal.

14

Looks like Naomi's bedroom. An elegant four poster bed with a couch at the end, as well as a seating area by the window. Gunther probably sleeps downstairs. An expressionist painting hung over the bed: a couple of naked women, as far as he could tell. Not my thing, he thought. Having caught his breath, he walked to the bathroom.

She was face down, but he recognized her. It was Bethann. He saw an outstretched arm and her phone just out of reach. He knew what he would find, but he felt for a pulse anyway. Nothing. "Stupid game," he muttered. Was the message 'Help! I can't brea...' part of the game? Or something else? She's only 62. Could have been a massive stroke, he thought. No need to jump to conclusions. Ed's training kicked in, and he took a few pictures of the scene with his phone.

As he sat down on the couch, he heard Naomi yelling from the bottom of the stairs, "This is my house, Bucket! Let me by!"

"Do as she says!" commanded Gunther.

"It's OK, Rusty! Let them up." Great, the two of them, Ed thought. Well, it is their house. "Can you keep an eye out for EMS?"

"Sure thing. Hey, one of the guests is ex-FBI, name's Mildred. Want me to send her up?"

15

"No! Ask her to get everyone's vitals," he called back down. "She'll know what to do."

"Prescott!" Naomi yelled as she reached the top of the stairs. "What are you doing? This is my bedroom! Gunther isn't even permitted up here!"

"She's right about that," said Gunther, following her in. "The sitting room is as far as I'm allowed!"

Ed felt his jigsaw puzzle calling to him. Oh, to be anywhere else, he thought. He looked over at Bethann. She deserves your attention, he told himself.

"A woman, a friend of ours, has died," said Ed.

"So?" Naomi countered. "People are always dying around here! That's what they do. Besides, it's just a game! A silly game!" Naomi nudged Bethann with her Gianvito Rossi platform shoes. "Get up, Bethann. Stop pretending!"

"Mr. Prescott," asked Gunther, "is she, is she really dead?" His face was ashen, like Troy's. Maybe he's human after all, Ed thought.

He heard commotion from downstairs. "EMS is here; they're coming up!" yelled Rusty. A young man and woman carrying equipment came up the stairs, "Excuse me Ma'am, Sir."

"Wonderful, more people! Look, Gunther, they're still wearing their shoes!" Naomi complained.

"Gunther," said Ed, "we need to go back downstairs.

Let them do their job." The host still seemed dazed; Ed shook him gently. "Gunther."

"Oh, yes, certainly we must. Prescott, my good man, can you help my wife? I'm afraid I need to sit for a bit. I shall be down forthwith."

"Sure," Ed touched Naomi on the arm.

"Unhand me! Never touch me! I don't even let Gunther..."

"Sorry, Mrs. von Hapsburg. Please lead the way."

Glancing back at Gunther, Ed was struck by how much older than his seventy-seven years he looked. This kind of thing ages a man, Ed thought. I know that only too well.

A Man of Substance

That annoying Prescott had left, and Gunther was now alone in Naomi's bedroom with the EMT's and Bethann's body. He watched the EMT's run through some kind of checklist. What is my plan now? Gunther wondered.

He remembered now when his Opa had given him a chess set for his thirteenth birthday. "Gunther, you are now a man," he had said while arranging the pieces on the board. "But more than that, you are a von Hapsburg man, a man of substance. Most men stumble and bumble through their lives, accomplishing nothing. A man of substance, he knows what he wants, he makes a plan to get it, and he executes that plan with cold, ruthless efficiency! You must decide, are you a bumbler or a man of substance?"

"A man of substance, of course!" replied Gunther.

Grandfather told him the rules of chess. He stared at

18

the boy intently, the clear blue eyes challenging him. "Let us play a game. Your objective is to capture my King. Now, make a plan and execute it! You have the white pieces. Make the first move!"

Gunther examined the board, looking for the plan. He remembered that controlling the center was important, so he advanced the King pawn two squares. His grandfather smiled approvingly, then slaughtered him within three moves. "That's called the Fool's Mate. You are a bumbler then," he pronounced.

Gunther felt the blood rushing to his face, coloring his northern European skin red. "Doch! I *am* a man of substance! I will defeat you at this game by Christmas. My plan is to learn everything about chess. I will execute this plan with cold, ruthless efficiency!"

Gunther checked out from the library every book on chess he could find. He continued to play against his grandfather over the next few months. Gunther learned from every loss. They played one final game. It was a late fall day, with light snowfall visible outside the window. Gunther made his last move and uttered the long sought after word–"Checkmate!"

His grandfather smiled, toppling his King. "Now, you are a man of substance!" They shook hands. Opa left, leaving Gunther to bask in his victory. Gunther realized now that his grandfather had had a goal also, to make him into a man of substance. Opa had executed his own plan with cold, ruthless efficiency, and he had succeeded. Gunther never forgave him for that.

From the bedroom, he watched the EMT's continue to work. He noticed Bethann's phone on the bathroom floor, just out of reach of her hand. Good God! He thought, our text messages! They're on her phone! I can't let anyone see those. Naomi must never learn about them. I need to have the phone! Gunther stood up and walked over to the body.

"Sir," said one of the technicians. "Please stand back."

"Please," said Gunther, putting on his best frail, old man imitation—his voice quivering and body trembling. "I, I just need to say goodbye to my dear friend. I have lost so many. May an old man do that?"

"Let the old man say goodbye," the other tech said. "We don't want another death." They stepped away, into the bedroom, chatting softly.

Works every time, Gunther thought. He kneeled down next to Bethann, the phone on the other side of him. "Dear Bethann, you were too good for this world," he sobbed. He picked up the phone and slid it into his pocket.

Standing up, he thanked the techs and went

downstairs. Now, for the next step in the plan. How do I get into her blasted phone?

The Interviews

Naomi stood at the bottom of her staircase. Horrified, she stared at the two parallel, greasy tracks down the center of her plush, peach toned carpeted stairs. The EMT gurney had also nicked a corner of the hand carved finial at the last turn before rolling out her front door. Good riddance, Bethann, she thought. "God damned low-class workers," she muttered through clenched teeth.

"Mrs. von Hapsburg," a velvety voice called.

Naomi turned and eyed the delicate features of Mildred Maxium. "I am Mrs. *Kahn* von Hapsburg." She traced her index finger along the ridges of her diamond choker.

"Oh. Thank you for clarifying." Mildred made a note in the pocket-sized notebook she carried everywhere. The habit had served her well during her FBI days. Who knew that in her own neighborhood, she would once again rely on notes to piece together the history of this crime. Well, a possible crime–murder, which is what some of the partygoers were murmuring. "I realize this is a troublesome scene for you."

"Of course! The tacky yellow crime scene tape is preventing me from entering my upstairs bathroom!" Naomi's indignant tone was unmistakable.

Mil cleared her throat. "Yes, well, there are some questions regarding what occurred here this evening. First, when did Bethann arrive?"

"Before the stated time. She always does...did." A bit flustered, Naomi paused.

"When did you initially see her?"

"I asked her to come upstairs as I put on my finishing touches." Naomi touched her own hair. "She agreed to help keep people out of my bedrooms, bathrooms, and closets. No reason for anyone to be anywhere other than the common areas. She agreed and went back downstairs. I remember, I was worried about those strappy stilettos on my thick carpet." Naomi blinked her heavy eyelashes and feigned a concerned frown. "She could have tripped."

"When did you notice Bethann again climbing the stairs?"

"Other guests required my attention."

"If this turns out to be an 'other than natural causes'

situation..." Mildred let the thought drift for a moment. "Can you think of anyone who wished Bethann harm?"

"Good Lord! She was loved by *everyone*!" Naomi said, her soft voice emphatic. A little too much loved by my own husband, she thought.

"I see. Did you notice any suspicious behavior or events during your party?"

"Well, there was an odd exchange between Troy and Bethann."

"Odd?"

"To be exact, it was more of a body language glare. He to her." Naomi coyly raised her chin just a notch. "I am quite good at picking up on those subtleties based on my years in Hollywood."

Mildred ignored the boast and thanked Naomi for her input. Noting in her little book, 'Mrs. H. a bit too eager to cast aspersion and suspicion on others.' She surveyed the room for another interviewee.

Ed followed Gunther into the study, escaping the commotion in the rest of the home. The host appeared to have recovered some after the shock of Bethann's death.

"How are you holding up?"

Gunther closed the heavy mahogany barn door behind them. "Thank you for asking, Prescott. I am doing well enough. It is quite terrible. Please sit down."

He indicated one of the substantial leather chairs facing his teak desk. The desk was covered with papers, neatly stacked and arranged, held in place with an acrylic paperweight. The stone inside the paperweight glinted gold in the light of the desk lamp. Nothing is too ostentatious for Gunther, thought Ed. "Sure," he said as he sat down.

"Would you care for a scotch? I do believe I need something to quiet my nerves." Gunther retrieved glasses and a bottle from a desk drawer. He poured two glasses and handed one to Ed.

"Don't mind if I do. Thanks."

He rose slightly from the chair and reached over the desk to take the glass from Gunther. Ed had many years of practice reading upside down. You never know what you might learn, he thought. The old eye injury made it more difficult now. Nonetheless, he glimpsed some papers having to do with property law and deeds. There was a document with an official-looking seal. Scotts County Deeds? Another was some kind of assay report? Probably nothing. He filed it away for future reference and settled back into his chair.

"Certainly," said Gunther. He quickly removed the

documents from the top of the desk. "My apologies. I am typically not so disorganized."

"No worries." Ed took a sip of the scotch. It went down smoothly; the man had good taste. "I am sorry to be asking you questions now, so soon after finding Bethann. Do you mind?"

"Yes, I quite understand. How may I help you?"

"How well did you know Bethann?"

"Not well at all. You see, I would not normally have an association with such a person, but she was attracted to me. I tried to dissuade her."

"Are you saying that Bethann was romantically attracted to you?" he asked.

"Certainly, yes," said Gunther. He shrugged his shoulders and smiled. "In a rather naïve way, you know the type. She endeavored several times to garner my attention, in rather obvious ways. She was not a subtle person." He attempted a knowing wink. "You realize, of course, that someone of my stature would not be inclined to reciprocate such feelings, as our stations in life were so far apart."

What a pompous ass, Ed thought, clenching his teeth to maintain control. "Yes, I can see that would be troublesome," he said. "How did you deal with it?"

"I simply explained the facts to her. I certainly

understood how she would be attracted to me. The gap in our social status was too great, I told her. She should disabuse herself of any such notions."

Ed took another sip of the drink. "How did she take it?"

Gunther frowned and said, "Not well, I'm afraid." He paused and met the detective's gaze. "My goodness! Surely, she would not have been so devastated!"

"Let's not get ahead of ourselves. I'm sure this was simply an accident." Ed stood up, looking at the now-empty desk. He's hiding something. But what? Deeds, property law, an assay report? Probably nothing. "Thank you for your time, Gunther. I'll see myself out."

###

Mildred went in search of a glass of water, her throat was dry from the excitement, and all the talking. Before she could reach her goal, the anxious look of two people coming her way caused her to pause.

"Excuse me," Mildred said, stepping in front of the couple who appeared to be on their way out. The woman's bag wiggled, and she spotted the furry tip of a tail peeking out from the oversized straw bag. The man behind her paid no attention and stopped short to avoid a collision.

Something yipped inside the jostled bag.

"Watch out!" Kitty snarled at her husband over her shoulder. The man mumbled something, eyes narrowed.

"Excuse me, I don't believe I've gotten to speak with you yet." Mildred tried to sound casual, sensing that a woman like Kitty required a light touch, not commands. Rusty and Kitty exchanged glances before nodding their assent. Mildred motioned to the armchairs in the corner. She pulled up a footstool to sit before them, sinking slightly.

"How well did you know the victim?"

The couple looked at each other again. Rusty leaned his elbows on his knees and folded his hands between them. His gaze dropped to his shoes. Kitty raised her chin, resting her fingers lightly on her collarbone.

"Not very well. Not much at all, I would say. She, well, how to put this? I didn't know her from anywhere. I mean, I saw her practically everywhere I went. She was in most clubs with us," Kitty paused, as if waiting for Rusty to jump in. When he remained silent, she continued. "What I mean is, I saw her around but didn't talk to her much."

"What about you?" Mildred asked.

After a beat or two, Rusty looked up. "Me?" Mildred nodded. "Well ma'am, I didn't know her either. Not even a lil bit..."

"Sure you did, well at least a little. That's what it looked like at TriPalooza a few weeks ago," Kitty chimed in.

"Look, honey, we were just in the drinks line together. That's all."

Kitty frowned. "It looked to me like you wanted to get to know her a whole lot better from the way you were laughing and pawing her."

"Darlin, I wasn't *pawing her.* I recall puttin a friendly arm around her shoulder, that's all. We were laughing about the Italian club party the other week. 'Member when Charlie started howlin the solo from Figaro, off-key?" Rusty's pitch rose with protest.

"Ok, fine," Mildred broke in, hoping to head off the marital meltdown that was clearly building up a head of steam. "Where were you when you heard Troy shouting that Bethann was dead? Were you together?"

"I don't know where she was, but I was loading up my plate with hors d'oeuvres at the time. Why, I prett'near dropped my blessid plate when y'all started screechin," he said, looking at Kitty.

Mildred turned to Kitty. "And you?"

"I, uh. Let's see, I was outside. Yes, Xena had to go potty," Kitty said. "When we came back in, it was chaos. Everybody running this way and that. It upset my widdle

29

pumpkin," she said, reaching into her bag.

Mildred jotted a few notes. As she wrote, she rolled her eyes up to glance at the couple. They were locked in some sort of silent exchange, though she couldn't tell much more. Rusty had a question on his face, and Kitty glared back.

"Thank you for your assistance. Any information will help sort this out all the sooner," she told them, rising and stepping aside to let them continue on their way.

Mildred had saved Troy Danville for last. She glanced at her notebook, nearly full. Should have gotten a bigger notebook, she thought. He looked shaken, the way most people looked after seeing a dead body. He had a drink in his hand. She had noticed him going to the bar several times as she had been taking other statements. Mildred had heard that Troy had a problem with drinking—a happy drunk at the Forge Bar. It's amazing how fit he still looked in spite of that, if it were true.

"Hi Troy," Mildred said, "I'm sure that this has all been quite a shock for you, finding Bethann like that. Do you mind if I ask you a few questions?"

"Um, shure," Troy said. "But why are you asking all

these queshtions? I mean she jus died, right?" He set his drink down hard on a side table.

"I'm just trying to help out–ex-agent, you know. I'd like to walk through the timeline of the party with you. To get a feel for where everyone was. When did you get here?"

"Lemme see, not long after the invite said to get here. Rusty and Kitty picked me up at the Forge, and we drove down. Gunther let us in after we rang the doorbell. We had to listen to those damned chimes for an eternity." Troy seemed to be sobering up quickly, at least masking it well. He smiled, almost maliciously. "Rusty said we needed to do something about those chimes."

"So, what happened next?"

"Gunther told us about this stupid Murder Game. Stupid game. Whatever. We started in on some cocktails and snacks. Lots of people were wandering around. It was hard to even hear Taco Bell's Cannon. But those stupid chimes kept going off. So, Rusty and me–we fixed it." He winked, "I hacked it, I'm an ex-SEAL with a unique set of skills, after all. We left the door open. It was getting kind of close, you know, with all the people."

"Wait, what?" asked Mildred. That complicated things. Anyone could have come in. "What time was this?"

"Beats me. It's not like I'm always looking at my

31

phone. I'm not a kid, you know," he said, baritone resonating, "But it wasn't long after that when Ed showed up. He can probably tell you." He looked back down at his discarded cocktail. Considered it for a minute and picked it up again, and took a drink. "That's when it all went to hell."

Mil settled into a wider stance. "OK, so Ed showed up. What then?"

"Yeah, that was kind of weird. He was asking about Bethann, where she was, he wanted to know."

"Why was he asking about her?"

"Something about a text. Why don't you ask him?" He put the drink back down, empty now, looking around. Probably wants another one, Mildred thought.

"A text?" she asked. Jesus, it's like pulling teeth. I hate interviewing drunks. It's so hard to keep them focused.

"You'll have to ask him. He was all upset. Come to think of it, it was something about not being able to breathe?"

OK, Mildred thought, definitely noting that down. Need to talk to Ed later.

"I know this is difficult, Troy. But that's when you went upstairs, right? When you found the body?"

"Yes." Troy turned and found a chair. He sat down, looking paler now. "It was part of the game. I was supposed to find her, and I did. She was face down on the bathroom floor. I teased her about how good a job she was doing, method acting, you know. But she, she just lay there, didn't say anything. I've served in Afghanistan, so I know dead when I see it. After I yelled downstairs, I don't remember much. So don't push me."

Not surprising, Mildred thought. Can't really blame the poor bastard, though.

Troy finally flagged down a drink. "Here's to you, Bethann. May you rest in peace, stupid bitch," he said as he turned away.

Mildred noted that comment.

###

Other guests milled about on edge, not quite sure what was happening. Ed moved on to the next person in sight. In his experience, the high and mighty rarely had far to fall from their uppity lives to the petty level of jealousy. He scratched the second fold of his thick neck.

Exhaling, Ed closed his left eye. It had been slightly damaged from gunpowder blowback during his last case before his retirement from the police department. With his good right eye, he scanned his neighbors as they tried to look important and innocent at the same time.

Rolling his left shoulder back slightly, he lumbered over to Naomi. Old habits. He had worn his shoulder holster on his left side. His ribs still missed the weight of his weapon. Clearing his throat, Ed began, "Uh, ma'am, may I have a few moments of your time now?"

"Yes." Naomi drew out the word as she turned from the food ladened buffet. She took in Ed's rumpled appearance and half lowered her eyelids as she half tolerated his request.

Ed did not display a notebook, preferring instead to summarize interviews out of earshot of the suspects. If you couldn't keep a conversation in your head, you had no head for this murder investigation business. He patted his right cargo shorts pocket, reassured that his digital voice recorder was ready for later.

"Quite a spread you have here. Both your house and the snacks." Ed wondered why he had not been invited. "Mind if I try some of these?" His left hand hovered over a plump shrimp; its tail hooked next to the cocktail sauce.

"Well, of course, do." Taken aback, Naomi considered what civilized person called shrimp cocktail a 'snack!'

"So, how long have you been planning this event?"

Naomi was confused. "Why would you ask that? Why does it matter?" She charged ahead with a seemingly

34

rehearsed answer. "The event," she spat out the word. "I prefer to think of it as our soiree, had its logistical details planned for seven weeks. The ridiculous Murder Mystery Game was my husband's bit of brilliance tossed in just before the invitations were sent."

"Word travels fast in this neighborhood. More time means more people knew about the gathering." Ed took a bit of pleasure both in the succulent shrimp and deliberately refusing to call a party a soiree. "Who might have shown up that wasn't on the invite list?"

"That damn dog, for one." Naomi, annoyed, pursed her lips and tossed her hair.

"No. I meant, could someone have entered without you or your husband noticing?"

"Unlikely. We upgraded to Westminster Door Chimes when the front door is opened. They do go on for a while..."

"So, only those people here now could have ended Bethann's life?"

"Are you asking me or drawing a conclusion?" Naomi crossed her arms and looked down at Ed. She loved the added height from her platform shoes.

Ed ignored the insult. "Where were you when you noticed Bethann was not on your main floor with your other," he paused, "guests?"

"I knew where she was. That stupid game of Gunther's would send folks upstairs, and I wasn't having that. Bethann agreed to guard my things. Oh my God!! That might be the answer! I need to go back up and check my jewels. She might have been protecting them. Why, I bet that's what happened. Someone was after my valuables, and she tried to stop them. That's your answer, mister detective. One of my neighbors is a jewel thief!" She moved to step around him to leave.

"Now let's not be hasty," Ed said, moving to block her path. She stopped short.

"Hasty? Someone might have stolen my jewels, and you call that hasty? Well, I never..."

"I'll let you go in just a minute. But first, I need to know if you have any idea what time it was when the shout came about the murder?"

"It was 8:15 pm. I know because Kookie, the caterer, brought in the dry-ice smoking cauldron of Jello shots exactly as I had planned. Usually, Bethann would have leaned over the cauldron with her cleavage showing and added some loud comment." Naomi stopped abruptly, realizing too late that she had likely allowed jealous acid to leech into her reply.

"Ah, now we know, even before the ME's report, a time range for the death. Thank you. Now you can go check on your things."

Naomi made an abrupt turn and headed for the stairs.

"If anything is missing, let me know!" he called after. Ed turned back to the buffet, thinking about Naomi's snarky cleavage comment. He decided Naomi might have planned more than Jello shots for one guest. He wandered upstairs to get another look at the scene.

Something outside attracted Ed's attention, and he turned to look out of the upstairs bedroom window. He saw a couple heading down the sidewalk. Someone he hadn't talked with yet.

"Damn!" he said aloud, turning to dart down the stairs. He tried to avoid the grease marks on the carpet, not wanting to grind it further in. By the time he yanked open the door, he was puffing.

"Wait, wait!" he yelled at the couple's retreating backs. They paused and turned. The quick motion caused high pitched barking from the woman's bag. It went on for a long time, and Ed resisted the urge to cover his ears. He shouted over the noise.

"I just have a couple of questions for you," he began. He was met by two stone-faced scowls. The man shook his head.

"Oh," said Kitty, "We already talked to the other one."

"The other one what?" asked Ed, looking puzzled.

"Your partner. You know, the lady cop."

Ed cocked his head. "Lady cop? Oh, you mean Mildred, she's a neighbor," he told her. Kitty staggered to the side momentarily, as a small white head appeared from her bag, followed by paws. She struggled to take hold of the wiggling mass of fur and lift it out.

"My poor widdle baby is so stressed out by all this nonsense," she exclaimed, clutching the animal to her breast.

"Whatever," said Rusty, shouldering his way in between his wife and Ed. "We already said our piece, and have to be gettin' on now, so y'all have to pardon us."

He stepped back and turned toward the street. "Please," asked Ed, "Just one minute, I promise."

"Ow!" Kitty yelped as she turned her ankle while losing her battle to hold onto the miniature dog in her arms. "Fine then, get down if you want to," she said, placing the dog on the lawn. Immediately, it squatted, releasing a powerful stream of urine. Ed hadn't thought such a small dog could hold so much in such a tiny bladder.

Rusty, looking alarmed, grabbed his wife by the arm

and pulled her a couple of steps in his direction.

"Go on, get that thing. We're leaving now," he said.

"But—"

"But nothing. I told you before, we got nothing to add," said Rusty, herding his wife before him like a sheep as they walked to their golf cart. Ed followed them for a few steps, thinking he might still persuade them, but they sped away in the cart before he could utter another word. Ed shrugged his shoulders and headed home to summarize his interviews.

Gina burst into the den, breathless, and saw Ed, head down, bent over the top of his desk. "You'll never guess what I heard? Someone died tonight at some party! Right here in Trivolity!" He raised his tired head and sat back in his chair.

"You don't look surprised. You know?" she asked. Ed nodded.

"How? I thought you were home working on your puzzle. You said you were determined to finish it tonight."

"I was but...Gina! How did you hear about it?"

"On the bus, coming back from the theater. All of a sudden, up and down the aisle, one cell phone lit up after the other as people got the message. It was an awful way to end a theater night. The play was so much fun, so many wonderful songs and dancing, and then... Wait! How did you..."

Ed swiped his hand over his face. "It was across the street."

"Oh, my God! At the von Hapsburgs? Their big exclusive party?" Gina's eyes widened. "No..."

"Bethann stopped by before the party to see if we were going. She was incensed that we hadn't been invited. I calmed her down, and she left to go over there. A little while later, she sent me a strange text. You know how she loves to kid. Well, I decided to go over and make sure she was okay."

"You went over to the von Hapsburg's party uninvited? I'll bet Naomi had a fit when you walked in. So Bethann was there? What does she think about all this? Did she tell you who died?" Ed stared at Gina, saying nothing.

"Oh No! No! No! No!" Gina shook her head and sank onto the only other chair in Ed's office. "Not Bethann! It can't be! Why would anyone kill Bethann? Everyone loves her!" Tears trickled down Gina's cheeks.

Ed came around the desk and wrapped Gina in his arms. "That's what I'm going to find out."

"How, Ed? How did she die?"

"Paramedics said it looked like natural causes. We have to wait to see what the Medical Examiner thinks. But..."

Gina looked up into Ed's eyes. "You don't think it was natural causes, do you?"

"I don't know. We'll wait for the report, but in the meantime," Ed moved back around to his chair and sat down, "we interviewed all the guests just in case it's more than that."

"We? Who's we?"

"Mildred Maxium. She's retired FBI. She was at the party and offered to help. Do you know her?"

"The name sounds familiar. I'd probably know her if I saw her. You know how bad I am at names."

"She'll be coming over tomorrow to compare notes. You'll meet her then." Ed turned back to the notes he was reading when Gina came home.

"Don't we keep the family accounts in that notebook?" she asked.

"Yeah, but it was the only paper I could find when I got home." Ed looked up. "Sorry. I was trying to get everything down while it was still fresh in my mind."

"Are you sure you should be doing this again after all you've been through? I'm worried about you, Ed."

"This isn't some stranger in a walk-up apartment on the other side of town, Gina. This is a fellow Trivolity resident and our friend. Besides, I can't ignore my instincts." Gina looked long and hard at Ed.

"How many accidental deaths that weren't 'accidental' have I seen, do you think? I can't point to why, but something is definitely off," he said.

"And what about the local police? Shouldn't they be handling this?"

"The Sheriff's department didn't seem all that interested; said they might come back in a day or two when they can—and here I'll quote—'spare a man.'"

The First 48

It was near midnight when Mil returned home, exhausted. She kicked off her shoes at the door, padded into the kitchen and poured herself a glass of Limoncello she'd been saving for a special occasion. If having to whip out her FBI skills at a party of neighbors where one was murdered wasn't special, she didn't know what would qualify. With her drink in hand, she sank onto her couch and opened her trusty notebook.

The first name noted was Ed Prescott, the retired Cleveland homicide cop. He had jumped into action and taken charge after the body was discovered. Protocols were followed, so he seemed to know his stuff, but who is he, Mil wondered? She needed to know his background if they were to work together, which they most definitely needed to do if Bethann's death was indeed a homicide.

Mil looked at her cellphone, noted the time, and

dialed Supervisory Special Agent (SSA) Dennis Castlebury. Being FBI, he was used to accepting calls at all hours of the night.

"Hey, Mil, I was about to call you," Castlebury said.

"You were?"

"Yeah. Got a call from Ed Prescott. Said he was a retired homicide cop working with you on a murder case? Is that true?"

"We were at the same party playing a Murder Game, no less! Little did we know we were playing with fire. Ed stepped in and took charge."

"He must be some cop to take charge over you!" Castlebury laughed.

"Very funny! So, what can you tell me about him? I want to know who I'm working with." She could hear Castlebury chuckling on the other end of the line.

"I thought you'd never ask!" Mil heard him take a drink before continuing. "What would be logical," Castlebury said, "would be for you to ask him yourself. I get that you want an unbiased opinion, so when you do sit down to talk, ask him about the First 48."

"The TV show? The homicide one?"

"The very same. He was on one of the first episodes with his partner. They were in the squad car. You'll see him in some fleeting shots, but you hear his voice throughout."

"Camera shy?"

"You'd have to ask him that. Maybe he didn't want to be seen, didn't want his wife and kids to be affected, or his career. But here's the thing, Ed's the star. Not the partner."

"And the partner?" Mildred asked.

"Dancing David Davis!" Castlebury laughed.

"You're kidding."

"Nope. You know, old triple D. Davis loved being on TV; loved being seen by his wife, his many, many children, and especially those women he already knew in the biblical manner. And, of course, the multitude he wished to convert."

"Triple D. Huh? I know the type," she said.

"We all know the type. But in the episode, you hear Ed's voice, then Davis turns to the camera and repeats what Ed said. It was mainly a step-by-step logical investigation, peppered with Ed's insights that broke the case...he's a natural born investigator."

Mildred let that sink in before continuing. "Did you guys work directly together?"

"We did. Back when he was a detective in Second District Vice. Vice squads at the time had carte blanche, gambling, auto theft rings, drugs, and even some white-collar stuff. And, of course, large-scale rollouts, you know those operations where you need all hands on deck."

"How well I know. Multiple search warrants, multiple arrests," Mildred said.

"Ed and I worked on a gambling case together. The Pittsburgh mob sensed a vacuum in Cleveland and moved to take over the numbers racket..."

Mildred cleared her throat as she tapped her foot rapidly on her faux wood flooring.

"Look, I'm prattling on. I worked with him in the field a couple of times. When I came back as a supervisor, some of my squad worked with him. I can tell you he's good police. A real team player. I trusted him. He helped me off the books. He trusted me. I helped him when I could." Castleberry paused. "Even the accident didn't change him."

"Accident?"

"His eye. The reason he retired early. You don't know this?"

"Hey, I just met the guy tonight, and we didn't get time to chat."

"Well, the firearm qualification for the Cleveland Police Department is a one day thing. You only have to shoot once a year."

"Only once a year?"

"It's not like the bureau. The standards are much looser. If you've put in over five years on the job, you just have to show up one time, with your duty carry, and fire 20 rounds on the range. You don't even have to hit the target. You could discharge your weapon in the dirt in front of you. Then you're off to the bar for the rest of the day."

Mil reflected on the hours she spent at the range; for required qualification, sidearm and shotgun, and all the extra practicing to become an expert. "Only once a year?" she said. "That's crazy!"

"Yeah, process that. Sadly, I don't think it is atypical for a lot of Police Departments. My understanding is it's a union thing."

"You'd think liability alone..."

"Yeah. Anyway, Ed was a good shot, came out and practiced on other days, and occasionally showed up at our office's open shoots."

"His eye? You said he injured his eye?"

"The story I heard was that he was at a qualification event and his duty weapon... I don't know what it was then, something semi-auto, whether a Glock, Sig, or Smith & Wesson, doesn't really matter... was having problems. The magazine or maybe the cartridges weren't sitting right. It kept jamming. The range officer took the weapon back to the shop to try and figure out what was going wrong. While waiting, Ed decided to use his partner's gun."

"Triple D," Mildred said.

"You know it. Fourth round in, while target shooting, the weapon backfired, damaging his left eye. It required surgery and rehab. After six months of medical leave, he made it back to duty but lasted only a week before pulling the plug. I guess he no longer felt safe out in the field."

"The department gave him a ninety-five percent injury pension, which was some money, but he was probably five to ten years away from full retirement. To make up the shortfall, they brought him on as a retired annuitant, a contractor working out of their cold case unit. Mainly unsolved homicides. And then put him on rape kits."

"Rape kits? Why rape kits?"

"There was a huge backlog of untested kits. Several hundred, maybe over a thousand, going back decades. Ed helped write up a request for funding for a federal grant. They got the money. The State of Ohio Forensic Lab started testing. When the results came back, match or no match, he and someone from the unit, usually a female officer, contacted the victim. Or, in the case of death, the victim's next of kin. Gave them the news, tried to get a statement to help build a case, and forwarded the results to the county prosecutor. It is really depressing work. A couple of our recent retired agents are working for the county on unsolved rape cases, and they are shattered."

"So, Ed...?" Castlebury had given Mil what she called for. It had been a long night, and she was trying to stay awake.

"Yes, so Ed retired, as did his wife; she was a nurse at The Cleveland Clinic. They decided to get out of the Cleveland weather."

"Have you talked to him since he moved?"

"When he first moved down there, he asked if I would be a reference when he applied for his North Carolina Private Investigator license. Sure, I said. We chatted then. He sounded good, really happy. Didn't hear from him again until he called about you."

"Why a PI license, do you think?"

"Well, he said, 'just in case.' Nothing concrete. 'Just in case.'"

Mildred thought for a moment, then asked, "Anything else I should know?"

"I did get a strange call from a county sheriff's department down there, checking the reference for his license. This may or may not be something to look into. The guy calling, and I could look back on this if needed, find the name, but the guy calling did not seem impressed by the FBI, federal law enforcement in general, the federal government as a whole, or Northerners coming down there playing cop. He let me know this in no uncertain terms. So, I'd be circumspect in my dealings with that office."

"Thanks, Castlebury," Mildred said, "for the information and for letting me interrupt your sleep."

"No problem. Always glad to help. Good luck with your murder investigation. Let me know how it goes."

"Will do!" Mil yawned as she hung up the phone.

The Phone

Naomi left for her spa appointment. No keeping a good woman down, Gunther thought. A failed party and a death in the house, and she soldiers on as if nothing happened. It was just one of her many endearing qualities.

Gunther entered the 'study' they had fashioned from the so-called third car garage. He never did any actual work there. Just as his wife had her upstairs retreat, he had his. By a tacit understanding, neither invaded the other's space.

He turned on the light and closed the door behind him. The simple room had a sofa, a desk, and an elegant chair, all of which had been in the von Hapsburg family for generations. Ah, the sofa—the location of so many happy trysts with Bethann. The furniture comprised the last remnants of the von Hapsburg legacy. That would have all changed if silly Bethann hadn't managed to get herself killed in Naomi's bathroom, of all places!

He placed the brandy snifter on the desk and sat in the chair. The bottle was from his private stock. Even Naomi didn't know about it. He thought wistfully of the times he and Bethann had shared a few glasses. Such a waste of good brandy, he thought, and glanced at his Tag Heuer watch.

Gunther unlocked the desk drawer and removed Bethann's phone, placing it on the desk next to his laptop. He plugged the phone into a charger, and the screen lit up. She smiled back at him; she had, of course, used a photo of herself for the lock screen. That woman had been her own favorite person, after all.

"Now the contest begins," he said with confidence. He had watched several YouTube videos on how to break into a phone. Mostly, they were no help, and Gunther wasn't the most technical person. He would never sully his hands with such things; that's why other people existed, such as janitors and the like. He could see no other way, though. How hard could it be for a man of substance with a plan?

I'll try her birthday first. We celebrated it on May 7th, but what year was she born? Well, she was 62, so do the math! Gunther entered 0566...invalid PIN, four more attempts before phone lockout!

OK, what next? She mentioned not having children.

That made his plan to marry her and get the land back less complicated, no pesky heirs to deal with. Her home street number, maybe? He entered *5555*...invalid PIN, three more attempts before phone lockout!

Damn, I'm running out of attempts. Wait, I remember seeing her sign in to the phone. She didn't use numbers; she drew something on the screen. Pattern lock, the obnoxious young punk on the video called it. What did she draw? It seemed funny at the time. Yes, it was 'bA'. Was that 'bA' for Bethann, or 'bA' for Bad Ass? Either way. He drew the pattern, and the phone unlocked. Gunther breathed a sigh of relief and took a congratulatory sip of the brandy. He opened the message app and frowned as he was not the first on the list. Inconceivable! Troy and Rusty had more recent messages.

Ed
I can't brea
Daniel
(picture)
Troy
You bitch
Rusty
So what

Maryann

Please call..

Gunther

Let them...

Who's Maryann, he wondered? But best get down to business. He clicked on his name and reviewed the messages:

Gunther - Sweet darling, my love, when can I see you?

Bethann - We must be careful dearest, love of my life, heart of my heart - people are starting to notice!

Gunther - Let them! I care not for the trifling rumors of the masses! Our love is all that matters.

And so on. "Such a waste," Gunther said, and sighed deeply. If only I had been able to execute my plan earlier. Naomi would be dead, Bethann would be mine and the land—the land would once again belong to the von Hapsburgs! Of course, it would have been satisfactory if Bethann had died afterward. However, no use dwelling on spilled cabernet. He deleted all of the messages between them.

The messenger app refreshed. So now, Troy and

Rusty, but who is this 'Daniel'? I really shouldn't look at them, he thought. But you never know what information might be useful; my career in advertising taught me that. Knowledge is power. Besides, I'm curious.

He brought up the messages. Hmm, pictures–fine looking young man. Could that be Troy's son-in-law? Yes, I remember Troy introducing him when I saw them at the mailboxes. He and Troy's daughter, Margot, were staying at his home for some reason. I'm sure they told me why, Gunther thought. But honestly, why bother remembering details about such people? Opa would have identified Daniel as a bumbler immediately. He read the messages, anyway. What could Bethann have seen in him?

Bethann - Oh, Danny. You are such a cutie! I enjoyed last night sooo much!

Daniel - I have never felt the way you make me feel! When can we meet again? I must have you!

Bethann - Soon! Maybe you can send me something to tide me over? You know what I mean...

Daniel - I thought you'd never ask :) I've been working on something just for you.

What could that be, he wondered. A poem? A work of pottery? Such a love-sick puppy. Gunther looked at the picture. My goodness, is that? He didn't send that, did he? Who does that? What kind of man sends pictures of his...parts? Well, it is impressive. He took a long swallow of the brandy, burning on the way down. She never asked me for anything like that, he thought.

He moved on to the messages with Troy. What could they have been texting about?

Troy - this is last time! No more! I swear - I'll tell Margot myself. No more money and you will stop seeing Daniel!!!

Bethann - oh, calm down, Troy - don't give yourself a heart attack! Yes, this is the last installment. But I kind of like Danny - he has some very nice attributes...

Troy - you bitch! Leave him and us alone! Or else!

So, that explains Troy's behavior at the party, Gunther thought. Bethann, you really knew how to make enemies. If you had come to me, we could have made such a great team. What a waste!

Now on to Rusty... This is turning out to be so entertaining! It may also be profitable.

Rusty - so what, I don't care what you say - no one will believe you.

Bethann - don't be so sure - I think a lot of people suspect already....

What's that noise? thought Gunther. Oh, it sounds like the garage door. Naomi must be back. Too bad, this was getting to be quite enlightening. Bethann touched so many lives. After connecting the phone to his laptop, he downloaded the messages and contacts. Gunther deleted the messages and wiped the phone clean. He turned it off and locked it in the desk drawer.

Plenty of time to investigate all of this later. When I get a chance, he thought, I'll return the phone to the bathroom and hide it in some corner. Let the cleaners find it next week. I can say the EMT's must have accidentally pushed it there as they worked on poor Bethann.

What's the plan now? Never mind that, what's my objective? What else is on the phone? What can I use? And who the hell is Maryann?

A Murder Board

The next morning, Ed woke early. Over his cup of coffee—he liked his coffee dark and unsweetened—he finished dictating the witness statements from the summary notes he had written after the interviews. Over his second cup, he reflected on his conversation with Castlebury from the Cleveland Office of the FBI. Getting the lowdown on Mil made him feel a little more confident going forward; it never hurt to have some sense of who you might be relying on.

By the time Gina awoke, came in, and kissed him good morning, he was scrolling through photos from last night's crime scene and selecting the ones to print.

"Hard at it already," she said.

"Well..." Ed started to say, then stopped. He always loved the way his wife looked in the morning.

"It's fine, it's fine, it is who you are." Gina squeezed his hand.

"Dennis Castleberry says hello." Ed paused. "He gave me the skinny on Mildred."

"I think I met Mildred? Mexican Train, maybe? Or some class? Until last night, I did not know she was a retired Feeb."

Ed grinned. "That's a term I haven't heard in a while."

"You've called them much worse, from time to time."

"True that. Not the good ones." Some FBI agents believed Copernicus was wrong, that the sun revolved around them and only them.

"Speaking of time," Gina said, "I have to get into gear. I've a Pilates class this morning."

When they had first moved to Trivolity, Ed began using the camera on his phone to snap photos. He had documented their house being built, their neighborhood in various stages of completion, and the surrounding trees and wildlife. The former detective paid attention to the birds at the feeders in their backyard. They were so different from the ones up north. He shared, probably over-shared, the photos with his kids. He could imagine them thinking, 'Oh great, another bird photo from Dad.'

On Ed and Gina's first Christmas Day at the new house, his wife and kids gifted him a state-of-the-art camera and a high-resolution photo quality printer. Over the course of the years, the camera had migrated into a desk drawer, and he found himself relying, once again, on his phone. Last night was no exception. It gave good results; the crime scene and party photos were sharp and clear. Ed narrowed it down to the photos he wanted. Pleased with his prioritized selection, he started to print the photos from last night.

Crime scenes are a funny thing. Ed shook his head in wonder at a thought he had often had. You walk through them and try to memorize all the details. At the same time, your mind is trying to solve the puzzle of who, how, and why. Your own photos and those of the crime scene tech, if and when one finally shows, document the scene. Later, you can use the photos to return to the mindset of that initial walk through. Sort through for things overlooked or review the space evidence occupied. Blood splatter patterns, smudges, heck, an endless list. Some might be used as evidence in a trial. Back in the day, Ed recalled using a Kodak Instamatic and those drugstore paper box cameras. It never hurt to have extras, film, or cameras in your bag.

As the photos came out of the printer, the retired detective spread them atop his desk. Reaching into the center drawer, fumbling around by touch, he found what he was looking for: a magnifying glass. Between his reading glasses and the magnifying glass, he could see crystal clear detail, in spite of his injured eye.

The doorbell rang. He could hear Gina answer and make small talk. Ed looked up to his wife and Mildred standing in the office doorway. "Good morning. Come on in," Ed said, his voice placid, as he pointed to a chair in front of the desk.

"Good morning," Mildred entered the room, a folder in hand.

Smiling, Gina said, "Nice to see you again, Mil. I have a class." She turned to leave, adding, "You two kids play nice."

"Have a good class, hon," Ed replied.

Rather than sitting, Mildred placed the folder on the seat of the proffered chair, went over to Ed's side of the desk, and began looking at the photos. "Nice quality," Mildred said.

Ed nodded. "Thanks. So, eh, Mildred..."

"Mil's good, just not Millie," Mildred looked up briefly. "I had a supervisor once who used it as a club. Mildred or Mil," Mildred looked up briefly, "either's fine."

"Right, I know the type. Okay, Mil it is." Ed paused. "Mil, I found out we have a friend in common back in Cleveland."

"Yes," her head still down, looking at the pictures, "He

seemed to think well of you. I mean, Dennis spoke well of you." Mildred pointed at a photo. "That photo, can I pick it up?"

"Sure." She gently picked up the photo of Bethann; her lifeless body collapsed on the rug in front of the bathroom vanity.

"That's how you found her?"

"Yes."

"Can I borrow the glass?"

Ed handed over the magnifying glass. Inspecting the photo, Mildred said, "I'm looking for any indication of something out of place. See, there in the corner of her mouth. I guess it could be saliva or maybe something left over that she was chewing or..."

Ed said, "I know what you mean. I took a sample."

"Huh?" Mildred said, looking up. "A sample?"

Reaching into a desk drawer, Ed held up a plastic sandwich-sized bag. Inside, through the clear plastic, a Q-tip with one discolored swab was visible.

"Ed," Mildred said, "I'm impressed."

"Allow me to temper your expectations. There were Q-tips in the bathroom, but no plastic bags. After taking that picture and other pictures, I took a sample with the cotton swab, but I had to wrap it in a tissue. I put it in the plastic bag later, after I got home."

"Still, there would be identifiable traces..."

"Let's hope so. I put the tissue in another baggy, just in case anything bled through."

"Still impressed," said Mildred.

"What's in your folder?"

"Ah," Mil said, "witness statements, photos taken at the party that were posted live online from all the social media accounts that I could find. Not sure I know everyone. They, the postings, all have time signatures. I, ah, I mean, we can build a probable timeline."

Ed shuffled through the photos, the brightly peppered statement, a fold out timeline printed or neatly drawn on graph paper. "You've been busy."

"No busier than you." Mildred looked around the den. Desk, bookshelves, desktop computer, printer, framed photos, all normal but personal and crowded. "I think we need a base of operations. Somewhere we can work uninterrupted and have a big board to display..."

"A murder board."

"Yes." Mildred paused, holding up the photo of Bethann, "similar to the one you did for the timeline, but with room to add what we learn about each suspect."

"I'll get right on it," Ed said.

"And we need to interview those who were at the party again. Maybe catch them unaware, at the pool, the bar, or at an event," Mil added, bouncing a little on her toes.

"Great idea!"

"I'm heading up to the club. Maybe if I'm lucky, one of the suspects will be there." Mil picked up her notebook and coat and headed out the door.

Rumors at the Club

It was a typical Tuesday. Residents were going about their business of living the good life at Trivolity. Only three days after Bethann's death, some neighbors were beginning to wonder if it really was a natural death.

Naomi stood in front of her trifold, full-length mirror, and tossed her hair over her shoulder, admiring its newly styled shape and body. Her mind swirled as she surveyed her image. The mock-opal crusted sandals picked up the royal purple-toned leggings and glinted in the fall morning sun. Her 70's retro colored blocked top had been custom ordered with inner support to lift, separate, and wrap tightly all of Naomi's torso assets.

Sauntering to her make-up table chair, she sat and pulled open the lipstick drawer. Briefly focusing on the twenty-three named tubes, she chose and applied Mysterious Mauve.

How appropriate, she thought. Still no definitive answers to the Bethann business. Naomi's spidey sense for gossip was registering a high buzzing. She could hardly wait to absorb the scuttlebutt in the 9:00 stretch class. She tightened her woven headband and picked up her gym bag, colored coordinated towel, license, and keys.

She was about five minutes earlier than usual. No sense rushing and working up a sweat. Naomi's exercise philosophy was stretch and tone. Foolish to work hard enough to waste a perfectly good makeup application.

Naomi's regular corner group of ladies seemed to freeze momentarily as she walked in. Words left hanging in the air as the women turned toward her.

"Oh, you poor dear! What a traumatic interruption at your party! How are you?" None of these women had been invited. It pleased Naomi that they were very aware of her soiree.

Not allowing time for an answer, another of the women said, "We heard it happened in your upstairs suite. That must be unsettling." Naomi remained silent, only responding with a demure smile. She learned long ago that empty air made people nervously fill in the conversational gaps.

Another woman voiced a suspicion. "Someone said that the outside caterer was not happy that Bethann intended to block Kookie's bid for the New Year's Eve dessert table." Naomi raised an eyebrow slightly. She had been wondering whom to thank for so cleverly taking care of a potential Gunther domestic mess.

"As horrible as this sounds to say out loud...one less entrapment concern for our men!" The group snickered in agreement.

Finally, Naomi spoke as the class began. She reached both her arms overhead. She then proclaimed with a royal tone and lifted chin, "We must all continue with our lives."

Meanwhile, Gunther eased into the warm, soothing waters of the hot tub, careful to keep his watch above the water. His thoughts focused on how his plan to get the mineral rights of the Trivolity land, formerly owned by the Cook family, had collapsed upon Bethann's death. He moaned a little. Someone passing by might have thought it was the lukewarm hot tub water, not a plan gone awry.

"They really need to repair the thermostat again," he grumbled out loud.

When he'd seen the Cook name on the club 'kitchen', he remembered Opa's story—how the Cook's had swindled Gunther's family out of the land. His grandfather had charged Gunther with getting it back. After spending time at the County Deeds office, he had come up with a plan. He had learned Bethann was the sole heir of the property, though he didn't know why.

Finally, he'd realized that there was a way to accomplish his goal—to get the family land back—the land Trivolity was built on, the land the Cooks had stolen from his family and sold to the builder. Naturally, he needed a plan to get it back, and the deed showed him the way. A clause in that deed meant that the mineral rights would revert to the Cook family once the last home was built. The gold Gunther knew was on the property would be his once he married Bethann. Wooing and marrying her would be a trivial matter. The only thing standing in his way was Naomi.

Naomi had been a fine wife, at first anyway. But now that they were both retired, she was becoming increasingly tiresome and expensive. Those spa treatments weren't cheap. The solution was simple. Gunther smiled at the *solution* pun. Just a mix of mouthwash and cyanide. Then he'd be free to marry Bethann. Kill two birds, so to speak. Sadly, that did not go according to plan. Now he had a mess to clean up.

"Ahhh! Nothing like a hot tub to soak your worries away, right buddy?" said a male voice already settled into the far end of the hot tub. Gunther winced as he didn't appreciate being called *buddy* by anyone, but he managed a weak smile in return.

"Got an opinion on what really happened to that gal over on Mirror Avenue who dropped dead at that party?" asked that same voice, who then added, "Heard she was only in her early sixties."

Gunther replied, "I don't gossip, my good man."

"Hey, don't get in a lather, buddy! I just heard that there might be more to it, like she wasn't that popular, you know what I mean."

"No, I certainly do not! Good day!" Gunther climbed out of the tub and went to the chaise lounge to retrieve his towel. He realized he needed to do something with that damned phone. With all these rumors and those inept, so-called investigators snooping around, it was imperative to keep one step ahead. But for that, he required more information. He wondered if there was something he could use from that phone to pin the tragedy on someone else.

As they walked in the door, Rusty thought, man, this place is hoppin! The parking lot was deceiving, because it had not looked that full. Kitty glided through the second glass door he held open for her, as she demanded he do, and trotted off immediately to join a group of women. Knots of people dotted the Capacious Chamber just inside the front door, and Rusty glimpsed customers standing three deep at the restaurant's bar.

He was a regular at the Club and was on the premises two or three times a week for one reason or another. The young woman at the concierge desk smiled a welcome. Walking past the fireplace, Rusty ventured down the hall past the Crow's Feet, where he saw the usual Thursday night Kegs and Cues group meeting for their weekly game. A football game on the screen behind them occasionally drew their attention, but mostly they leaned on their cues and chatted between shots. Rusty recognized Troy and raised a hand in greeting.

Kitty had disappeared into the crowd as she worked her way around the room, darting from one gathering to another. Rusty made his way to Cook's Kitchen without her. She knew where the Wine Dinner was, so he did not need to hold her hand like she was a child, though he thought she sometimes acted like one.

Only a few people graced the well-appointed room. The staff had outdone themselves, transforming the cozy nook from a casual gathering place to a handsome, elegant dining establishment. Tables were draped in cloth and laid out with formal tableware and beautiful place settings. Servers in matching uniforms roamed the room, pouring glasses of champagne to welcome the guests as they arrived.

One group had shoved their two tables together, ruining the effect of an upscale restaurant. Rusty wondered why some people never seemed to be able to go anywhere without their clique in tow. Events like wine dinners were great opportunities to meet new people, but some in Trivolity insisted on treating it like high school, refusing to associate with anyone beyond their own little group.

Rusty selected an empty table and smiled at the approaching server. "Yes, champagne would be great, thanks, and some for my wife too," he said, tilting his head at the empty seat to his left. After a few moments, a couple he did not recognize sauntered over and asked to join him.

"Certainly, welcome y'all. My name is Rusty, and my wife Kitty should be along shortly." He stood and grasped the stranger's hand in a warm double-handed shake.

"Bert and Gracie," the man answered as he pulled out the chair for his companion and then seated himself on Rusty's right. They accepted their glasses of bubbly and looked around the room.

"Not many people here, I'm surprised," murmured Bert. Rusty was unsure whether the comment was meant for him, but he answered anyway.

"Not yet, but it'll fill up in a minute or two. I noticed the bar was doing a brisk business when I walked in. I'll bet you that mor'n a few people attending this dinner stopped at the bar first."

Bert looked confused. "Why would someone do that? Didn't they look at the menu and realize each of the five courses is matched with a glass of wine?"

"Y'all would think so, but for some folks, these things are less about tasting new wine than an opportunity to drink as much as possible." Rusty grimaced. He enjoyed a good, strong cocktail occasionally as much as the next person, but he also believed in moderation. All those years in business had made him wary of losing too much control in social settings.

As if on cue, a large gaggle of people made their way past the windows and seemed to want to fit through the double doors all at once. The staff snapped into action, steering people to open tables. Kitty straggled in at the rear and snatched a glass of champagne from the nearest server on her way past. Her 'fairy hair' sparkled as she moved under each light in succession.

"Hello there! Kitty Bucket, nice to meet you," she said to her tablemates, shaking their hands in turn. She removed her napkin from its ring with a flourish and sank down beside Rusty. "How long have y'all lived here?" she asked.

"Going on four years now," replied Gracie, shifting in her seat to face Kitty.

Rusty glanced at the women and thought they seemed

compatible. He drained his champagne and perused the printed menu the staff had laid on the charger in front of him. Had he not thought it impolite, he would have licked his lips. Many of his favorites were listed: Hawaiian poke, spinach salad with glazed pecans, berries and goat cheese, PEI mussels in white wine, and roasted shank of lamb. The only item that did not appeal to him was dessert, since he was not a sweets man. No matter, Kitty would snarf down the flourless chocolate torte. He was so absorbed in his food fantasy that Bert's voice startled him.

"I don't think we've met before, which seems odd."

"Yeah, a little." Rusty said, "We likely run in different circles."

"Did you hear about the party where someone died?"

"Yes, sir, I surely did. In fact, I was there," Rusty replied, hoping he didn't sound boastful. Information was valuable currency around the community, and reputations were made and broken in the exchange.

Bert leaned forward in his seat. "You were! What really happened?"

Rusty related the basics of the party to his companion, including guests and the general theme, ending with the paramedics taking the body. He didn't mention the sleuthing taken up by the two ex-law enforcement officers.

"Oh, I know Troy, he lives two houses down from me.

I saw him just the other day. Funny, he didn't mention anything."

"I'm not surprised. It was...upsetting for most of us who were there."

"You said it was Bethann Cook who was found dead. Is that the same woman who volunteered to give prospective residents a tour?"

Rusty shrugged. "I think I did hear something 'bout that, but I'm not for sure. I don't think we have too many here with that name. It's not like Deborah or Mary. We're swimming in those." He made eye contact with a server and called him over for a refresh on the champagne.

"Well, if it was," continued Bert, "Troy certainly didn't have a high opinion of her."

"How so?"

Bert leaned in closer to Rusty. "I forgot who told me," he said in a low voice, "the woman was, what do they call it these days...a cougar. She put the moves on Troy's son-in-law, Daniel, who lived with him here for a time. Troy was grousing that instead of looking for a respectable job, the kid was spending all his time chasing 'afternoon delights' with Bethann." Bert exaggerated a wink.

Geez, how old is Bert? Who winks like that anymore? thought Rusty. "Isn't that interest'n," he replied, "When you say kid..."

"Oh, I think he's forty-five or so. I only met him briefly once." Bert sat back to make space as the dinner service began. The room was full and buzzing.

"Don't do it, Troy. You'll scratch for sure!"

"Shut your pie hole," said Troy. "I can make the shot." It felt good to be back with the guys playing pool. Finally, he could relax and have some fun, now that the problem had solved itself. The Crow's Feet was packed, both pool tables taken, and players waiting their turn. He took a last sip of his scotch before lining up the shot.

"I just need to apply a little English to the cue ball, and I won't scratch. Watch and learn, rookies!"

Troy hit the cue ball on the side, and it collided with the eight ball at the perfect angle. He watched as it headed to the side pocket and fell in just as he called it. He then saw the cue ball meander down to the other side pocket. Don't you dare, he thought. It hovered at the edge...and fell. "Well, shit!" Troy smacked the edge of the table with his flattened hand.

"Damn, sorry about that. Scratched on the eight ball." He fist-bumped his opponents while his partner headed off to add their names to the list of players waiting. "I guess I have time for another drink."

Troy made his way into the packed Forge bar. Wine dinner tonight, he remembered. He saw Rusty heading into Cook's Kitchen and waved at him. Rusty and Kitty frequently attended these dinners. Rusty took a seat at one of the tables, but Troy didn't see Kitty. He wondered where she was.

Probably freshening up, so to speak. Others were getting tanked up at the bar before tasting the carefully selected wines at the dinner. He gestured at the bartender for another scotch and water, top shelf of course. The barman knew Troy's usual.

"Um, Dad, how many is that? Three? Four?"

He noticed his son-in-law, Daniel, sitting at the bar. "None of your goddamn business!" Troy growled. His daughter Margot had probably asked her husband to keep an eye on 'the old man'. Daniel was good-looking, but Troy suspected from the beginning that the marriage was going to be a disaster. Margot was too trusting and was taken in by Daniel's smooth talk and big dreams. There was no talking her out of it, no point in even trying. Thank God her mother Julie had passed on before all this mess happened.

"Are you keeping track, little man?" Troy asked, oozing disgust for his son-in-law. "Look, I'm just enjoying myself. I can finally relax. You have no right to criticize me after what you've done! And you're going to tell Margot that

I've only had one glass of wine. Got it?"

Daniel looked back down at his drink. "Right," he said softly.

"I can't hear you! Do you understand me!" Troy jutted his face within inches of Daniel's.

"Yes! Dammit!"

"Good." Troy took his drink and went back to the Crow's Feet. There was a chair open by the poker table, turned so that people could watch the pool game while waiting their turn. He sat down and watched but was drawn into a conversation going on next to him, which he couldn't help overhearing.

"Did you hear about Bethann?" the guy next to him asked his companion.

"Yeah, I heard something about her dying at the von Hapsburg's party. What have you heard?"

"Nothing much, I don't get invited to such things, too low class for them. I guess it was natural causes, maybe a stroke or something. Although she was kind of young."

"Yeah, that seems weird. You know, after someone dies, you start hearing all kinds of things. She was really popular, but it seems some people didn't like her."

"Really? She seemed all right to me, a real looker, too."

What do they know? Troy wondered. He had thought

that Bethann's death would be the end of his troubles. But could the secret still come out somehow? I need to know more, get ahead of things. If there's a rumor about Daniel and Bethann, I need to kill it. Why couldn't the kid just keep it in his pants, for God's sake?

"Hey," Troy said. "What have you heard? I thought everyone liked her, too."

"Nothing much, just that Rusty really hated her. He tried not to show it. But as I hear it, she had something on him. He seems to be much happier now that she's gone."

Hmm, Rusty, Troy thought. Too bad, I like him. But this may come in handy if the investigators come snooping.

Lessons and Libations

Mildred found Troy in the Crow's Feet. He was playing pool alone. She said hello as she walked over to the cupboards holding the shared book library and perused the selections. She pulled out Central Park West and set it on the poker table. Ought to be good for a laugh, she thought. There were two glasses on a side table. One was empty.

"You're Troy, right? We talked after the party."

He looked up from the table and gave her a once-over, evaluating something, as if doing some mental calculation. Mildred knew that his wife had passed away some months ago. Maybe he was trying to decide if she was worth his time. Single men had a lot of options at Trivolity. At least they thought they did. She had to admit he was good-looking and seemed to be in excellent shape for his age.

"Yes, I remember," he replied, smiling. The

calculation must have resulted in her favor. "I apologize for not recognizing you when you came in. Mildred, right? May I call you Millie?"

Why? Why do they always want to use that awful nickname? She wondered. Control, of course. Well, let him think he has control, then. "Sure," she said, nodding at the pool table. "I always thought it would be fun to play pool. I keep thinking I should show up for Kegs and Cues on Thursday nights, but I'm afraid I would just make a fool of myself."

"Well, Millie, you just need a good teacher, that's all! And you are in luck. I just happen to have some time on my hands. Would you like a lesson?"

"That would be great! Let me buy you another round to pay for the lesson. What are you drinking?"

"That's generous of you, but sure—an Old Fashioned."

"I'll be right back," Mildred said, thinking that's not all he's looking for. When she returned, Mildred set the drink next to the two empty glasses and set her house red down as well.

"OK. I'm all ears," she said, standing with hands on hips.

"So, pool is, to begin with, a straightforward game. It's a matter of geometry," Troy began, in his 'radio announcer' baritone, happy to have an audience to regale.

"I've taken the first shot The break, as we call it. You see, there are solid colored and striped colored balls. We take turns trying to sink a ball in a pocket. If it's a solid, that person needs to sink all the solid balls; the other person needs to sink all the striped balls. Finally, when a person has sunk all their balls, they need to sink the eight ball without scratching–that's what it's called when the cue ball drops into a pocket. Let me show you how to shoot."

Troy handed her a cue and pointed out the six ball. "If you see where the cue ball is, you can visualize a line that connects it to the six ball, and you can see an angle that connects the six ball to the side pocket. That's the angle at which you want to hit the six ball. Hey, you're an ex-cop, right, Millie?" Troy glanced Mildred's way.

Mildred gritted her teeth, holding off on her usual comeback. He was putting her in her place, she knew. A cheap trick to belittle her. Let him think it's working. "Ex-FBI Agent, actually."

"Of course you were, so you know all about how to line up a shot, when you need to take someone out, right? You can't miss. Hey, have you ever had to?" He stared intently at her, weighing her. "I mean, take the kill-shot?"

"No, thank God. I don't think that I could live with myself. You?"

"Yes, a couple of times in Afghanistan. It was nothing

personal, just a job to be done." Troy shrugged one shoulder dismissively and turned Mildred so that she could hold the stick, pointing it at the cue ball. She felt him behind her, wrapping his arms around her, placing his hands on the cue, just behind hers. The dominance game, again, she thought. "Here, let me show you. Hold the stick like this. Your right hand next to mine at the back end, and thread the skinny end through the fingers of your left." She felt trapped by the way he held her. She knew the type, aggressive but weak. "Now, push the stick through your fingers and hit the cue ball."

She did as he instructed; the cue ball collided with the six ball at the proper angle, and the six ball fell into the side pocket. "Perfect!" he said, releasing her from his hold, but not before his right knee unnecessarily pushed the back of her thigh.

"Thanks!" Mildred replied, feigning her happiness at the lesson, relieved to be freed from his embrace. He downed the Old Fashioned she had brought him. I haven't even touched my wine yet, she thought.

"Now, lesson number two. Do you see now how you are set up perfectly to sink the four ball? Not only did you make your shot, but you are now set up to make another. Always think about your next shot."

"Thanks, I will."

They continued to play until only the eight ball was left. Now, Mildred thought, it's time. "Hey Troy, did you see the posts on Facebook from the party?"

"No. Don't do Facebook. Too much drama for me." Bunch of whiny, spineless people, Troy thought.

"It's just that, you know, I've heard you didn't care much for Bethann."

Troy lined up the shot. "Didn't care much one way or the other. Don't get me wrong, I'm sorry she's dead. Now, pay attention. I need to sink the eight ball to win. But if I scratch, I lose."

"OK, but there's a photo of you at the party," Mildred said as he pulled his cue back, preparing to shoot.

"Yes, and?"

"Well, you are handing her a drink, like a Martini..."

Troy shot. The eight ball went in, but he hit too hard, and the cue ball followed it in, scratching. "Fuck!" he said, throwing his stick down. He glared at her, then. She could feel his anger rushing at her. The back of her neck prickled as she recognized how capable he was of being dangerous.

He stood breathing deeply for a moment, then reached down and gathered up his cue. "Sorry, that was uncalled for," he said, smiling again like he was flicking a switch. "So? I gave Bethann a drink. Nothing to it, really.

It was an open bar, after all. It was a party, so I thought I should be friendly. As I said, I didn't think much of her one way or the other. Oh, I just remembered, I am supposed to meet my daughter. Maybe we can continue the lesson later?" Troy turned on one heel and marched off toward the bar.

"Sure," replied Mildred. "I'd like that," to his retreating back.

"Hello Ed," said Mildred. "I had a nice chat with Troy."

Gina had just let her into his office, where he was reclining back in his easy chair regarding the murder board.

He pushed his glasses back onto his forehead and smiled. A genuine smile, not like Troy's. "Hi, Mildred. A nice chat, eh? I like Troy, but I always get the feeling he's hiding something. Some kind of tension below the surface."

"You wouldn't be far wrong. He's not someone you want to cross. The kind of guy who's your best friend one minute, then he'd slit your throat the next. Of course, he'd be real discreet about it and nothing personal, as he would say—almost a borderline sociopath, I think."

"Well, it's not like he'd be the only one of those in this neighborhood," Ed waved at the other chair in the room. "Please sit down. Did Gina offer you anything to drink?"

"No, I'm good. I just had a glass of wine at the Forge. I bought Troy an Old Fashioned to get him talking. By the way, do we have an expense account?"

"Sorry, you're not working for the Feds anymore. This is the Trivolity Bureau of Investigation—not the FBI."

"TBI, huh?" Mildred shot back. "Snappy title. What you mean is we're on our own."

"You got it," laughed Ed. "So, did you learn anything from Troy?"

"Well, he taught me the finer points of playing billiards."

"Good teacher?"

"Considering that I was district champion three years running, no. But I asked him about the photo of him handing Bethann a drink. I thought that was an odd thing for him to do, given what Naomi had said just after the party." She consulted her notes. "Here it is: 'body language glare'. Anyway, he freaked out but got his composure back pretty fast. Even so, I think there's something there."

"So," Ed said, "we have a photo of her heading

upstairs with the drink..." Mildred saw a red dot illuminating the photo on the murder board.

"A laser pointer, Ed? Really?"

"Sure, the guys gave it to me when I retired. They even engraved it. See–DCUWCY."

"What the hell does that mean?"

"Don't Call Us, We'll Call You. Hah! I miss those guys. Anyway," he continued, now aiming the laser at the photo of Bethann in the bathroom. "There's no glass here. But..." the laser moving on to a photo of Rusty coming down the stairs. "There's a drink glass in this hand. I can't say for sure, but I think it's empty."

"Wow," said Mildred. "What are you thinking? Troy poisoned her, and Rusty's getting rid of the evidence? Some kind of cleaner? You think they're working together?"

"Maybe. I'll see what Rusty has to say for himself tomorrow. He's giving me golf lessons. Unlike you with pool, it's been a while since I last played a game. I'm a little Rusty." He grinned.

Mildred stood in front of her narrow, full-length mirror and sighed. These feminine self-pampering days were a waste of time and money. If women really wanted to keep themselves fit, it was simple. What they put into their mouths, how often they moved, and whether they kept their thoughts on a positive level mattered more than creams, steams, and massages.

Still, trapping Naomi in her self-centered world might be fun. Mildred saw her own amused smile and then tipped her head to loosen her usually tight chignon. Dark hair swished gently around her shoulders. The length made her appear taller than her five foot ten inches. Her olive skin accentuated the delicate scar that ran under her left rib cage above her flat belly. The mark was just long enough to end any two-piece bathing suit dreams. That final FBI drug bust chase was halted by the incident with the snitch. Damaging her kidney and future career choices. "Yeah, well, here I am again, sleuthing in my own neighborhood." She tightened the belt on her wrap around dress.

Mildred carefully zipped the small duffle containing all the items she imagined she might need for a day of moaning while sipping red wine. Of course, she could not take her trusty notebook into the spa rooms, but her keen memory would suffice to store any tidbits Naomi dropped regarding Bethann's demise. Mildred felt curious and confident as she pulled up to the Spa building.

Inside, Mildred shared a twenty-dollar bill and some news with the desk clerk. She and Naomi had a lot to chat about. "Would it be possible to have a private room for the scheduled services? Thank you so much." Mildred settled in face down on the massage table, felt warm pebbles being placed on her smooth back, and listened for Naomi's usually grand entrance.

"Oh my! I did not realize this was a tandem room." Naomi slid onto the empty table and pressed her shoulder blades flat on the pre-warmed towels. "Ahh," she exhaled as her spine soaked in the warmth. "I suppose it is for efficiency that they have two people receiving different treatments in the same room."

Inwardly, Naomi seethed at the intrusion. However, she was determined to enjoy her well-deserved pampering. Mildred, not wanting to reveal her identity just yet, only murmured an agreeable "Uh huh," to the floor.

"Well, in any case, I certainly can use the relaxation time after this awful week." Mildred held her own lips tightly together as she thought, well, unlike Bethann, you are still alive.

Aloud, Mildred only rolled out a "Really?"

"It isn't every week that you become the center of attention because someone died, was likely murdered, in your upstairs bathroom!" Naomi managed a tone both indignant and teasing.

Mildred maintained her monotone reply pattern with,

"No, who?"

"Bethann Cook. Although I did not include her in my circle of dear friends, she was fairly visible around here. She seemed to take on any 'interactive position' available, if you get my drift. Besides, as they say, keep your friends close and your enemies even closer. When we built here, we were forced to endure her tour. She knew absolutely nothing about building or decorating style, for that matter."

Mildred was definitely catching the venom drifting through the conversation. As she felt the stones being removed from her back, Mildred knew Naomi was having an elderberry and pomegranate facial. The essence hung in the air along with fresh cucumber slices headed for Naomi's closed eyelids.

Mildred rolled over onto her side as thermal wraps were applied to her calves. "How well did you know her, and why would anyone want to kill her?" Silently, Mildred considered whether Naomi was clever enough to mention murder to lead others to assume she had nothing to do with the crime.

"For one thing, or should I say many things, she slithered around all the men, married or not. Even my dear Gunther, not the sharpest crayon in the box, seemed delighted by her attentions." Good grief, Mildred thought. Naomi must have had a few preparatory tongue-relaxing drinks before this spa session. "There was always something slightly saccharin in the sweetness of her speech," Naomi continued.

Mentally noting the reference to deception, Mildred thought back to her own deceitful courthouse visit. The clerk, who may have been under the impression that the former agent was in real estate, shared that in the last few months, several people had sifted through the same land documents Mildred requested. Specifically, a pompous man and later a woman who kept mentioning her paralegal expertise gleaned from work in property management.

From her table, Mildred pressed Naomi for more information. "Who stood to gain by Bethann's death?"

"Who do you think you are?" Naomi spat out. As she sat upright, the two cucumbers launched from her eye sockets. "Oh, it's you!" Her eyes narrowed as much from the facial as from her fury. Time for my exit, Mildred thought, calmly removing the thermal calf wraps and striding purposefully out of the room. That was fun, she thought, as behind her Naomi sat rigidly, dripping fruit, hatred, and fear.

Ed slammed his door in the parking lot of the Scottsville Country Club. At least the weather's better than I expected, he thought, shivering a little in the early morning chill. His golf date with Rusty was hard-won, and he would've been loath to let it go, even if it had been raining. Which it wasn't, for once. He knew how to play golf but fully anticipated throwing his game. He'd heard Rusty was pretty good, even toying with the idea of turning pro back in high school. Perhaps that's what gave Rusty the edge as an executive, Ed mused.

The retired detective knew that putting Rusty at ease was paramount if he was to get him chatting about Bethann. Giving his 'mark' the idea he was easily winning at golf was essential. The trouble was that it would take Ed some time to figure out how to moderate his own game. He would just have to assume Rusty was quite good and go from there.

"Hey, buddy!"

Ed had just begun to turn when he felt a slap on his back, harder than he would've thought necessary. A cough caught in his throat. "Ah...pardon me.... Morning Rusty. Looks like we snagged a good morning for a game."

"Agreed!" Rusty bestowed a broad smile on Ed, grasping his hand in a double-handed shake. The detective smiled back, half as enthusiastic. They walked up to the office to check in.

"Are we walking or riding today, gentlemen?" The young woman staffing the counter asked them. Ed thought it was courteous of her to at least ask and not make an assumption. He chuckled under his breath, even though he believed the answer was obvious.

"Beautiful morning for a walk, don't ya think, partner?" Rusty said, not pausing for an answer before continuing to the clerk, "No cart for us today, honey."

"Any balls today for y'all?" she asked. Ed shrugged, still reeling from the shock that they would be walking, but Rusty shook his head. She took their payment and clocked them in. They exited toward the first hole, walking by the row of men and one or two women practicing shots on the putting green.

"What's new with you, Ed?"

"Not much. You know, a lot of my time recently has been sunk into this thing with Bethann."

"Thing with...oh, that's right."

On the fairway, they had to wait a couple of minutes for the first hole to clear, then they teed up. Ed let Rusty go first. The better to judge things. Rusty drove his first ball straight down the middle.

"Nice!" Ed told him. Rusty grinned. The detective lined up his ball, sighted it a few times, and tried to relax. It had been years since he'd actually played, and he regretted not suggesting they hit the driving range to warm up before their game. You're not here to win, he reminded himself, you're here to get some information.

Ed's first few shots were alright, then he took a couple of bad breaks and Rusty was soon leading. The next hole was par 5, and Rusty slammed it perfectly. Ed was less lucky, and though he swung with vigor, a brisk wind kicked up and his ball landed in a thick blanket of pine needles in the nearby trees.

"Too bad, man," Rusty said, sounding sympathetic, as they trudged down the hill.

"I'm probably too distracted. This investigation into what happened with Bethann has taken over my brain." He paused, hoping his partner would take the bait.

"Anything I can do?" Rusty asked, his wariness apparent to the detective's trained ear.

Ed nodded and stopped to catch his breath. "Yes, actually. I was wondering how well you knew Bethann. I knew her fairly well, you see, and considered her a close friend," he said, knowing that offering personal information first was often the way to get people to open up.

Rusty paused to root around in his bag for a cloth and proceeded to wipe down his wedge, trying not to let his face show his concern. He hadn't realized Ed and Bethann were such good friends. Good friends share things. How much did Ed already know?

"We knew each other from here and there. You know

how it is."

"I do. Except for people who never seem to leave their houses, it seems everyone knows everyone else. I guess what I'm asking is what you might be able to tell me that could shed some light on what happened."

Ed selected an iron from his bag and made a reasonable effort at getting his ball free from the spongy bed of needles where it rested. It didn't go far. He fell silent, waiting for Rusty to line up his shot. Disturbing a golfer prior to a shot was a mortal sin. The ball rolled dangerously near the trees that tightly lined the fairway, but in the end, it stayed clear. They walked. Rusty seemed to have forgotten Ed's question, or at least he was stalling. The detective would have to use information he didn't want to divulge to nudge.

"You both played pickleball, right? I seem to recall something Bethann said once about being confused that you were collecting dues. Do I have that right?"

Ed thought his golf partner's face paled, even under the steel gray sky. Rusty started to say something, stopped, then began again. "Yes, that's right."

"Well, maybe I heard wrong, since I don't play pickleball, but I thought Tim Sheriden was the treasurer, or was there an election I didn't hear about?"

Rusty coughed and shook his head. "No, yer right. Tim is the treasurer, but he was trav'ln for a time and asked me to help him out. You know, follow up with some people who might have forgotten their dues."

"Mm," Ed muttered, mostly to himself. "I see," he said, a little louder. Rusty came to a stop near his ball and set his bag down. The breathless detective set down his own bag, gratefully, just as he felt a fat drop of water smack him in the forehead. He looked up to see pewter clouds amassing over the course. The wind had played up, and the pines began to sway. So much for the forecast.

Dampness from the pouring rain had begun to seep through Mildred's jacket by the time she stepped through the door of the arts and crafts studio. She wondered if the weather had caused many people to stay home. To her surprise, the room was nearly full. She shook the rain from her mackintosh and surveyed the studio. Mildred saw one or two people she knew. The women were all chattering away happily, and no one glanced her way. There was one lone man, looking out of place and awkward. The only empty chair among the tables of four backed up to the clay press. It was difficult to get to, but Mildred squeezed through the narrow space and lingered by the chair. She waited a moment for a break in the conversation so she could ask if the chair was available, but no one took a breath, so she sat.

Mildred was mildly surprised to find herself sitting next to Kitty Bucket. What luck, I couldn't have planned it better, she thought. Kitty didn't notice her right away, but when she did, Mildred thought she saw a flash of panic as their eyes briefly met before the woman dove right back into the table talk. Mildred surveyed the pile of what looked like junk in the middle of the table. A six-inch clay pot sat before each person.

"Ladies, I'm sorry, ladies and our one gentleman, could I get your attention?" asked the woman Mildred assumed was the instructor. A few women ceased their discussions, but it took the leader several rapid claps of her hands to quiet the space.

"Thank you for coming. We're going to be making our own unique flowerpot creations. You'll find on each table a collection of items you can use to decorate your pots." The art teacher told them. She continued to explain the process of painting the pots, selecting decorations, and modge podging them in place. Mildred tuned her out. When did we all regress to kindergarten? she wondered. She'd signed up for the class because the description sounded interesting, not realizing it would take only preschool-level skills. Never mind, she told herself, it's a good chance to pick Kitty's brain about Bethann.

As the women worked, Mildred made small talk to

lure Kitty into meaningless conversation until the other two women were so deeply engaged with each other that Kitty was excluded. Then Mildred set to her own work.

"I'm still shaking my head about our poor Bethann," Mildred said, "Aren't you?"

"Um, yes, that was so...unfortunate."

"Did you know her well? You must have if you and Rusty were invited to the party."

Kitty reached for a section of wrapping paper and scissors. "Sorry, what? Oh, well, yes and no, I guess. She was in my book club, so I knew her from there, like everyone else."

"I don't follow," Mildred said.

"The book club, it's the biggest one we have here. The 'After Five Somewhere' club?" Kitty responded, sounding surprised.

"I'm not familiar. What kind of books does that club read?"

Kitty squinted at Mildred as if the retired agent had just said she wasn't aware that birds flew in the air. "Oh, we don't. The only thing you have to do is bring a book, any book, and a bottle of wine. The hostess provides the snacks."

"So...you don't all read a book, then discuss it?"

Kitty snickered. "Of course not. Well, every so often

we get someone new who tries to talk about a book they read, but we get sidetracked and end up just talking. Eventually, they give up, and either join in or leave."

Mildred nodded and felt a little sad that she wasn't all that surprised. "When was the last time you saw Bethann, before Naomi's party?"

"Ah...that probably would have been the book club meeting two weeks earlier." Kitty turned to look at someone walking their dog past the studio, then looked down at the large handbag tucked under the table at her feet.

Mildred followed her gaze and wondered if Kitty had smuggled her pooch into the art class. That dog certainly seemed to be an obsession. She recalled Kitty's statement that she was outside with it when Bethann's body was discovered. Mildred picked out a photo of some kind of animal from the pile and glued it onto her pot, not realizing she had it upside down, and the creature's legs jutted up towards the rim. Too late, she realized her error. Oh well, she reasoned, it's art.

"So," she restarted her conversation with Kitty, "You didn't have any sort of real relationship with Bethann then. No history."

Kitty frowned at her. "No, I told you. We were 'book club pals' and not much more."

"What about Rusty?"

"What about him?"

"Did he have a relationship with Bethann?"

Fury spread across Kitty's face. Mildred recalled the expression 'if looks could kill' but held her gaze steady on her companion. They eyed each other. Mildred knew that if she were the first to look away, any authority she had would evaporate like a mud puddle in a desert.

"Enough about that stupid woman already. She's dead. It's over," Kitty snarled.

"What's over?"

Kitty scooted her chair away from the table. Its legs screeched horribly against the floor, causing Mildred to flinch. "She is. Her life, all her affairs, whatever. Stop bothering me!" Kitty said as she reached under the table for her bag. She marched out the door, nailing Mildred with one last glare as she stepped outside. Mildred watched as Kitty scurried towards the parking lot, the rain plastering her hair to her head.

Ah, this is what a wine tasting looks like, thought Ed as he walked into the Annex. This is really Mil's kind of thing; too bad she's busy decorating flowerpots. So, count your blessings, Ed.

Gina said she had seen Gunther up here. The

detective forced himself to leave his house and come up to the club. He had to ask the concierge where the Annex was located. Just straight through the Forge, was the answer.

Ed saw what must be the tasting table after he rounded a corner of the main dining area. He walked up just as a couple was leaving with their glasses. The young man at the counter greeted him, "Hi! Welcome to the Uncorked Taste and Spit! Are you Uncorked?"

"Whaaat?" asked Ed. "Um, I live here. Oh, you mean am I a wine club member? No, I'm more of a beer and bourbon man."

"No problem, just five dollars on your member's charge."

Ed searched his wallet and couldn't find anything resembling a 'member's charge'. Fortunately, he had plenty of cash, as usual. He handed over a five-dollar bill.

The server took the bill, seeming not completely sure what to do with it. He shrugged and pocketed it. "If you are a bourbon man, I have a fine bourbon barrel-aged cabernet. I'm sure you'll find its complexity appealing."

"Sure, what the hell? I'll try it out." The young man poured the wine, filling the glass a quarter way up.

"You can do better than that, son. It's wine, not bourbon, and these old bones don't want to make too many trips back here." Ed handed him another ten dollars.

The server took a quick glance around and smiled, "Sure, here you go," he said, filling the glass to the top. "Enjoy! Here's the tasting sheet."

Right, thought Ed. It's red, and it's not beer or bourbon. What else is there to know? He saw Gunther sitting by himself in an overstuffed chair by a window. He was right where Gina said he would be, making notes on his sheet, occasionally glancing out the window. As Ed approached, he noted Gunther's frown and followed his gaze. The scruffy-looking guy Ed had seen pause outside of the party was now on the patio nearby, staring inside intently at Mr. von Hapsburg, who shifted uncomfortably.

"Hi," said Ed. "Is this seat taken?"

"No, that's fine. There's no one..." Gunther started and then took a sip of one of the four wines on the table in front of him. He took another look at Ed and said, "Oh, it's you. Prescott, isn't it?"

"Yes, that's right, Gunther. You can call me Ed."

Gunther glared. He doesn't like familiarity, Ed remembered. He had wanted a reaction, and he got one. But then, Gunther smiled.

"Sure, Ed. And Gunther is fine. After all, we were both good friends of Bethann. We should honor her memory and be friends, as well. What do you think?" he raised his glass.

Not what I expected, thought Ed. He returned the gesture, "To Bethann! She will be missed." They clinked the glasses together.

He took a sip of the wine. Wow, thought Ed, as the flavors of the bourbon barrel-aged wine hit his taste buds. I've never tasted anything like this! Wine, where have you been all my life? He finished the glass. "This is good shit! Now I know why people drink wine. What do you think a six-pack of this goes for?" he asked. Gunther didn't say anything; he just stared at Ed.

Is he having a stroke? Ed wondered. I can't have my prime suspect die on me before I finish my interrogation. "Gunther? Mr. von Hapsburg? Are you OK?"

"I. I. I've never seen anyone do that before. I have no idea what a...six-pack, they don't come in six-packs. I mean..."

"Are you sure you're OK? Do I need to call someone? EMS?"

Gunther turned away from Ed and took a sip of one of the wines in front of him. "No, I'm fine, really. This unfortunate incident with Bethann, I'm sure it's rattled all of us. Ed, you should really sip the wine, not swallow it all at once."

"Sorry, this is kind of new to me. I'm more of a beer drinker."

"Then why are you here?" Gunther asked.

Crap, thought Ed. Now he's suspicious. He ad-libbed quickly, "It's for Gina. Her birthday is coming up, and I wanted to pick out a nice wine for her." Not my best work, but maybe he'll buy it.

"Oh, I see."

"Yes. I can tell you know your wines. Any recommendations?"

"Gina's your wife, I remember now. You are a very lucky man, Mr. Prescott, err Ed. I have my beautiful Naomi, of course. She's pleasant enough. After a number of years, and of course, she's always there, always demanding..." Gunther paused and stared out the window again. "Bethann, you see. She was different, a lovely woman. If only...."

Ed felt acid building in his stomach. Should have had something to eat, probably should not have gulped down that wine. He vowed to stick to beer. It, at least, had nutritional value.

Gunther seems genuinely distraught. There's no way he would've murdered Bethann. The old guy had a crush on her, that's obvious. He wondered again at the effect Bethann had on men. Jealousy was a likely motive. Just how many men did Bethann have wrapped around her finger, and how many women had she pissed off?

Ed eyed Gunther over the rim of his near-empty wine

glass, remembering that right from the beginning, Gunther appeared truly horrified and genuinely shocked. After seeing him today, I think we can eliminate him from suspicion, he thought. Bethann's murderer is not Gunther. I need to tell Mildred.

Lay Of The Land

"There's way too much going on in and around the von Hapsburg's party for a death determination of natural causes," Mildred said as she came into Ed's office and plopped her stack of files on the desk.

"I couldn't agree with you more." He turned the murder board he'd prepared toward Mildred and rubbed the back of his neck.

Moving closer, Mil picked up a marker. Three names, Rusty, Troy, and Kitty, were in capital letters and circled. Deep in thought, Mildred, absentmindedly tapped the desk. She stepped forward. Her marker squeaked across the board, adding and circling Gunther's name.

"Do you really think Gunther would risk killing someone in his own home during his own party?"

"I didn't think so, at first, Ed, but I overheard a conversation that bears looking into, at the Forge where I stopped by for a quick lunch. Four women, sitting in the booth behind me had a very interesting conversation about the party and the von Hapsburgs. My back was to the gal talking the most. I couldn't help but overhear."

"Ed, did you know the von Hapsburgs had ancestorial ties to this property?"

"When you say, 'this,' what do you mean?" Ed took off his glasses and sat back in his desk chair.

"This!" Mildred swirled her arms. "The property this community is built on!"

"Seriously? How can that be?"

"That's what we have to find out. Apparently, the family back in the late 1800's had a land grant and then an estate here."

Leaning forward, Ed said, "What does that have to do with the von Hapsburgs?"

"That's the best part. Gunther, well I should say Naomi, is always bragging that her husband comes from Royalty. Well, the name of the lord who built that property is..."

"Von Hapsburg?" Ed said.

"Bingo!"

"Holy cow! I always wondered why Mr. High and Mighty bought into a community like ours. I know they built the biggest model and added features the rest of us couldn't afford, but still, why here when there are more exclusive communities?"

"Maybe there is something to what I overheard. According to the woman who did most of the talking, her husband was admiring an old map framed and hanging on the wall in Gunther's Man Cave. They'd gone there to smoke cigars and have a drink. Apparently, after several drinks, Gunther started talking about the property and how incensed he was with the way the land was stolen from his family. Then he winked at her husband and said he had a plan to get it back."

"What? Get it back? With all of us owning houses and living on it? He must be delusional." Ed said. "Are you sure you heard it right?"

"Oh yeah! The three other women started laughing hysterically! The gal talking became angry that her friends didn't believe her. They even suggested that maybe her husband had been smoking pot and misunderstood."

Ed folded his arms and scrunched his eyes, deep in thought. "You know, Mil. It wouldn't be that hard to check up on the history of the property."

"That's what I was thinking," Mil said. "I'll go to the Register of Deeds office in Scottsville tomorrow and see what I can find out."

"Registry of Deeds...." Ed shook his head. "That

reminds me. When I talked to Gunther in his study after we found Bethann's body, I noticed something. Yes, that's it. There was an official-looking document on his desk. It had a seal on it, from the Scotts County Deeds Office. I don't think he wanted me to see it. He cleared his desk real quick. Sounds like it's related." Ed drummed his fingers on the desk. "Something else is nagging at me. I glimpsed an assay report, too. That's to check on minerals, right, like gold. There's got to be a connection."

"Yep, could be something there. Still, I think we're missing something else, Ed. I can feel it."

"My thoughts exactly. The motives we've uncovered so far seem too obvious." He riffled through his notes. "We've got a victim who was loved by most of the residents I talked with and..."

"...hated by the rest," Mildred added. "Our victim appears to have had dual personalities, and one of those personalities pissed someone off enough to do her in. But who? And why?"

"And why do it at the von Hapsburgs? There's something here." Ed said. "We just haven't found it yet."

The Sister

It had only been a day or two but I was already on task, armed with my second cup of morning coffee, sorting through all the party pictures and the interview notes, trying to see what we were missing when Gina came in, holding out her phone.

"Ed, it's Allison," Gina said.

"Allison?"

"Allison Camp? From my Mexican Train group? You know her and her husband, Jack." Gina waited.

"Okay," I said.

"She wants to talk to you." Gina handed me her mobile. "It sounds urgent."

"Hey Allison," I said. "It's Ed. Something I can help you with?"

In a breathless whisper, Allison said, "There's someone in the house."

I sat up straighter. "There's a stranger in your house?"

"No. Not my house. Next door."

"Okay, so you're safe. That's good. And the person next door, your neighbor, are they home?"

"The person next door is dead."

"How do you know they're dead? Wait, Allison, who lives next door?"

"Bethann, she's dead, right?" Her voice got a little firmer. "Aren't you the one that found her? She was my next-door neighbor. And I'm trying to tell you; there's someone in her house."

"How do you know? Can you see them? Is there movement?"

"There are lights on, and someone walking around. I can see shadows through the curtains. Look, Ed, I thought you were interested in her death. I mean, I wouldn't bother you, but Jack's at pickleball. I didn't mean..."

"No, no. Thank you for calling. I'm headed over right now. Thank you, Allison."

I opened a desk drawer, grabbed my handcuffs, my retired badge, a small pepper spray canister, and my five-shot Smith & Wesson Chief and dropped them into my pockets. I called Mil and filled her in.

"I'll meet you in the drive," Mil said.

Handing Gina back her phone, I kissed her on the

cheek. "Gotta run," I said on my way out the door.

"Be careful," she said.

Mil was in the drive by the time I pulled up. "There's definitely someone in there," she said. "Let's circle the house. See if we can pinpoint a location."

Mil went to the west, I went to the east. The first-floor windows were eye level, the curtains mostly closed with a slight opening. Each room on the side was clear, but the kitchen and great room had light and a shadow moving. Mil and I met in the backyard. "Definitely someone in the Great Room," she said. The only way out through the back of the house was a three-paneled slider.

"Knock on the front," Mil said. "I'll cover the back."

I made it to the front door and rang the bell. After a five-second wait, the door opened, and there stood Bethann.

"Mil!" I shouted. "Mil," I yelled, louder.

We were at a sunroom table, waiting for our drinks, just Mil and me. "Weird," I said.

"Weird," Mil agreed. "Not twins, well, not fraternal twins. What was the term you used? Irish twins?"

"Yeah, born in the same year, nine months apart."

"Their poor mother," Mil said.

"When I was working in Cleveland, there was a set of Irish triplets on the job. A pair of twins and a brother born ten months later. Two detectives and a patrolman. Their old man had been on the job..."

Maryann entered the room with a tray of coffee, tea, and cookies. "This is what I could find," she said. "Sorry, there's no loose tea, just these bags."

"Looks great," I said.

Maryann bore a striking resemblance to Bethann. After getting over the initial shock, I began, however, to see differences. Maryann wore little or no makeup, and she had a shapeless dressing style. Bethann had been all about packaging, always dressed to the nines, everything lifted and tucked, as if she was waiting around to be discovered and cast on The Real Housewives of Somewhere. Maryann, nine months the junior, had on a faded tie-dye sunburst top, a free-flowing peasant skirt, and worn leather sandals. Her hair had the look of combed-out dreadlocks. I could see the smear of faded tattoos peeking out beneath her sleeves.

"We weren't sure who was in Bethann's house," Mil said, after introductions were made. "We appreciate your willingness to talk to us."

"No problem," Maryann said. "Besides, I knew you

were safe to talk to the moment I opened the door."

"How so?" Ed said.

"Your auras." Maryann nodded toward Ed. "Yours, Ed, is primarily green with purple around the edges, whereas Mil's is mostly blue. Both indicate positive energy I can trust."

"You don't say!" Mil said, intrigued.

"You actually see colors around us?" Ed was incredulous.

"Yes! I've been seeing them my entire life. They've helped me keep negative influences out of my life."

"Well, now I've heard everything," Ed said.

Hot drinks and cookies served, Maryann said, "I was shocked when the medical ex...exam, something like exam. Anyway, they told me my sister was deceased. The call came out of the blue. We weren't close." She looked around. "I was never in this house before."

"We're so very sorry for your loss." Mil asked, "How long has it been..."

"We called each other a few times a year. Birthdays. Holidays. So maybe the day after New Year's."

"Anything stick out?"

"She told me she had a few new boyfriends. I said at this point, I hope they're all man friends." She smiled and sipped her tea. "She always had a lot of guys hanging around, married or not. Both her and the men." She looked up, cleared her throat. "Fidelity was not her strong point."

"It's a beautiful house and very well kept," I said. The house, a Graham style, was like Bethann had been when alive, neat, nothing out of place. "And Bethann was well-liked, a nice person," I said. "She was a friend of ours." I sipped some coffee.

Mil said, "I'm new to this community and your sister went out of her way to make me feel welcome."

"She had her good points," Maryann said. "Growing up, we were a team, sisters against the world. Like the three musketeers, but only two."

We let that sit for a few moments.

"So," Mil said, "the Medical Examiner called you."

Maryann nodded. "Two days ago, late. I made arrangements that night. Came here straight from the airport. She had sent me a key, maybe two Christmases ago. Lucky I still had it and could still find it."

"Sorry you had to hear about this from the ME," Ed said. "I have to tell you, most people did not know she had a sister." Maryann's eyes filled with tears. Mil grabbed a box of tissues off the side table and offered her one. I put my hand on Maryann's other hand and squeezed as she dabbed at her eyes.

"You're both very kind," she said. "Thank you."

"Where did you travel from?" Mil asked.

"An ashram, more of a commune really, east of Albuquerque, in the Sandia Mountains. Working on myself. I've been there off and on for over a decade. Helping the community, meditating, farming, planting. Practicing Buddhism."

I nodded. "That sounds admirable."

"To be truthful, that's one of the things that separated us as sisters. Bethann was very materialistic. It was the most important thing to her. I was always a little more spiritual. From the beginning, I knew there was more to life than nice clothes and jewelry and flashy cars."

Mil nodded. "We're all on our own path, I guess."

"You know the saying, first time marry for love, second time marry for money? Bethann skipped right to the second and never looked back. Even in high school, nothing was as important in a boyfriend as the Do Re Me."

Ed said, "Woody Guthrie, right?"

Maryann smiled. "Yes. Bethann carried on like that her whole life: boyfriends, men friends, lovers, and husbands. Everything had a price tag. I guess I could understand at first. Our father got caught up in Ronnie Raygun's Savings and Loan crisis. We were teens when he lost everything and went to jail. We were forced to live with our mother's parents, who were mega-religious." She stirred her tea and then nibbled a corner of a cookie.

"That sounds like a challenging upbringing," Mil said.

"Sweetie, you have no idea." Maryann looked up. "I'm sorry. I don't mean to sound dismissive. All of this has stirred up a lot of negative energy."

I tried to look as sympathetic as possible. Mil seemed to do the same. Mil said, "No offense taken. It's a lot."

"Our grandparents were always harping on about Satan and all his traps and temptations. Our poor mother, it broke her to be back there, away from her new life, from her friends, her neighborhood, her wealth. She spent all her time in the old bedroom, resting, a wet washcloth across her forehead." Maryann fiddled with her cup, then looked at us and went on. "We had no one to defend us. Our older brother, Billy Dan, would have sided with us, but he was already grown and long gone by then. We were two teenage girls who could not dress or speak or listen to the radio or watch TV or do anything that did not open us up to God's displeasure. No wonder we rebelled. Boys, drugs, alcohol, the whole smear." Maryann stood up, went to the sink, and rinsed out her teacup. "I am going to use the ladies," she said and exited the room.

"Damn," I said. Mil shook her head, side to side.

After a moment, Mil said, "I noticed the office beside

116

the kitchen has a laptop open on a desk. We need the laptop to search Bethann's phone messages."

"Right. My thought is we listen, offer to help, and to organize. I mean, this poor woman was just dropped here out of nowhere. She does need our help."

"We could offer to take her to the ME, but we need her to ask for an autopsy. We can search through files and records to help, I guess, with the estate, to locate any pre-burial..." Mil stopped as Maryann returned to the room. She sat down again at the table and put her head in her hands.

"Maryann," I said, "we are so very sorry you have all of this to deal with. We are here to help you in any way we can."

Maryann said, "You both are very kind. I can feel such positive energy from both of you. It makes me trust...but the Medical Examiner..." she left it hanging in the air. "I don't know if..."

"That's not a problem," I said. "We'll be with you if you want." The appointment for the viewing and ID at the ME's office was scheduled for the next day at eleven. We offered to drive and stay with her during the viewing. "In the interim," I said, "what can we do?"

"There's so much to be done." Maryann looked around.

"If I have your permission," Mil said, "I'll take a look in the office and the computer. Search for anything she might have prepared in advance for..." Mil paused.

"For any unforeseen events," I said.

Maryann nodded. "Please."

"In the meantime, is there anything you need?" I said. "Something to eat or drink?"

"I think I'd like to lie down," she said and left the kitchen. We could hear her make her way up the stairs.

"You take the desk," Mil said, "I'll look at the computer."

The office, a room with two shaded French doors, had a stylish executive desk, a cushioned rolling chair, some small file cabinets, and bookshelves. Two curved back chairs faced the desk, for the illusion of guests, I assumed. Sepia prints of vintage flowers and leaves were framed on the wall across from the desk. The prints, desk, and shelves, the whole office, bore the taste of some designer. You could imagine it as a designed set from a glossy catalog, someone's idea of what an office should look like. The entire house had that vibe, curated and designed, with no one specific in mind. It all looked vaguely familiar, from the sitting room to the sunroom. Haverty's? Pottery Barn? "What's a step up from Pottery Barn?" I wondered, half aloud. "Restoration?"

118

"What?"

"I just noticed this whole house seems staged, all the furniture..."

"No personality." Mil said, "Not to over-generalize, but that's not uncommon around here. People finally have the money to buy what they want, but do not remember what they want. So, they let somebody else decide."

"Haverty's, Pottery Barn, not Ethan Allen anymore."

"Too much dark brown furniture."

"Of course, it doesn't apply to designer golf clubs or those second fantasy cars," I said. "Who needs a Lamborghini to drive to Walmart?"

"Apparently, a few of our neighbors." Mil smiled and got back to business. She looked into the drawer beneath the computer. It was filled with pens and loose paper. "Everyone in our age group," she said, "writes their password somewhere convenient, just in case."

I noted Mil had said in our age group, without a hint of irony.

"Heck, when I was with the Bureau," she said, shifting through the papers, "the in-house security officer would check our desks for our passwords. The number of written reprimands..." The computer was open and plugged in. She lifted it up and looked underneath it. There, on a yellow Post-it note, was the password. "What was her user's name?"

Pulling my phone out of my pocket, I checked my last message from Bethann—I can't brea.... "Try Bethand1, that's Beth, capital B, lower case e-t-h-a-n-d followed by the numeral 1."

Tapping on the keyboard, Mil said, "Bingo. We're in." Looking at it quickly, Mil said, "It looks like everything she did on her phone is backed up here. Photos, call logs, messages, everything." Mil made a few keystrokes. "We're in luck. All of her phone messages are automatically backed up. It looks like they are all here. It goes back years." The keys clicked. "And she has a FindMyPhone app." Mil taped some more. "I found where her phone is located."

I bent over, looked at the screen. "You're shittin' me," I said. Mil smiled.

"Let me make a call," I said. "I'll ask Gina to come over to sit with Maryann."

Someone cleared their throat. Maryann was standing in the doorway. "Would it be possible," she said, "to see where my sister died?"

"Sure," Mil said, closing the laptop. "It's a beautiful day. Let's walk. It will give us a chance to explain some of what we know took place."

Ed, Mil, and Maryann stood at the von Hapsburg's door waiting as the obnoxious doorbell went through a litany of tunes.

"Well now," Maryann said. "I've never heard anything quite like that."

Before Ed and Mil could react, Gunther answered the door. "Oh, how delightful," he said, frowning. "What do you want?" Ed and Mil parted so Gunther could see Maryann. Gunther gasped and stepped back, causing the front door to bang open against the large Blue Ming vase sitting in the corner behind it. "Bethann?" He croaked. "That's not possible." He stared, blinked, and stared some more. "What, how..."

"Gunther," Ed said, "meet Bethann's sister, Maryann."

"Maryann," Gunther stepped forward and offered his hand, trying to recover his composure, his face trying on a sympathetic look. "I am so very sorry for your loss." When their hands met, Gunther tried to pull her into a hug. Maryann arched her body backward, minimizing contact. Gunther had the look of someone who had taken a Viagra and was just told, 'Not tonight, Buckeroo, I have a headache.'

"Maryann wondered," Mil said, "if she could see

where..."

"Certainly, of course," he swept his hand in open greeting, "anything I can do. Please come in," Gunther said as he stood aside.

Without talking, they headed up the stairs to the hall and through the bedroom to the bathroom. All the while, Gunther was busy speaking in a low voice to Maryann.

Once in the bathroom, Ed turned and said to Maryann, "I found her here. She was on the floor. I felt for a pulse, but she was already gone."

Maryann started to tear up. "My poor sister." She turned and walked into the bedroom.

"Would that be all?" asked Gunther. "You know my wife refuses to use this bathroom, to use the bedroom. She doesn't want to be near..."

"So, she hasn't been in here?" Ed asked. Gunther shook his head. "How about you?"

"Well, once or twice. To clean up."

"You cleaned up?" Mil said.

"I mean, I was here, well, supervising when our cleaning lady cleaned up." He directed a challenging look at Mil, then Ed. "Why, is that a problem? The EMT fellow said it was fine."

"Did you notice Bethann's phone?" Ed asked.

"Her phone? Didn't you take it?" Gunther asked. "Or

one of the EMTs? Wasn't it in her purse? I think the EMTs took the purse."

"No." Mil paused, "There are, that is...we have indications it might still be in the house."

"Well, retired agent, I haven't seen it!" Gunther puffed up. "I'm not sure I'm comfortable with what you two are implying."

"We're not implying anything. That phone would be the rightful property of Bethann's sister. We just are trying to help her deal with all of this," Ed said. "And, I have to tell you, the last place I saw it was in this bathroom."

"Do you mind if we look around?" Mil asked.

Gunther said, "No, by all means. Anything I can do to help Maryann?"

"That's alright, we've..." Ed started. Reaching down, Gunther moved aside the wastebasket.

"Wait--" Mil said.

"Look what I found!" said Gunther. He brought his hand up, gripping the phone. He handed it over to Mil, as if called upon to present a trophy for 'First Runner-Up', and marched out of the room. "Maryann, you poor dear..."

"So much for fingerprints," Mil said.

"I guess," Ed said, "we should be happy he didn't lick it."

"How do we know he didn't?" Mil said with a grin.

Back at Bethann's house, Maryann went upstairs. I began again looking through the files while Mil scanned through the computer. In the desk, there were some papers and land maps in a file marked Heritage. I set it aside for later review, as well as a file marked Aquamation/ Donaldson Funeral Home. "Looks like she planned her funeral."

Mil picked up the file. "Water cremation? That's a thing?"

"Return to a natural state. Maybe the sisters had more in common than we knew." We dug back in.

"Have you noticed," Mil said, "how Maryann sometimes looks above our heads, as if there is something there we're just not seeing?"

"Now that you mention it. I thought it was an eyesight thing, like resetting your focus. But I did notice it at Gunther's. She looked long and hard."

"I'll bet she was checking his aura and not liking what she saw," Mil said. "I'd love to know what colors surrounded Gunther."

"Does scum have a color?" Ed asked.

Maryann appeared in the doorway. "About tomorrow. Are you still planning to go with me?"

"Of course," I said as Mil nodded.

"That's good, thank you."

"We think," I said, "that your sister's death was not from natural causes."

"Yes," Maryann nodded. "I know."

"An autopsy would really help, Maryann. We can't ask. The request would have to come from you," Mil continued. "You need to be the one to ask."

"Yes," Maryann said.

"I'm a licensed NC Private Investigator and Mil will be assisting me under that license," Ed said. "We'd like you to hire us to investigate."

"You mean a PI? Like in the movies? Down these mean streets type of thing?"

"I see the ashram has access to TCM," Ed said. "It's really not that dramatic. With Mil's background in the FBI and mine with the Cleveland PD, we know how to talk to people and fit things together."

"Of course, you two have been nothing but helpful."

"Tomorrow, I'll have a contract for you to sign. I'd say it's free, but that might invalidate our confidentiality privilege. We have to settle on a fee."

Mil said, "How about one dollar, American?"

"I can swing that," Maryann said.

The Condolence Casserole

Naomi heard Gunther enter through the side door and then move into his man cave office. Harrumph, she snorted. I bet he is trying to hatch a new land grab scheme. He may not be brilliant or original, but determined, oh yes. Apparently, the end of Bethann was not the end of things.

Naomi needed a counter plan. To verify the existence of the surprising sister, Maryann, she needed an excuse to enter Bethann's house. Ah, the Southern Parade of Condolences Casseroles was likely to begin immediately after the neighborhood realized there was a visitor in Bethann's house. For Naomi, cooking was out of the question. She decided flowers and a gift card to the Hot Coals Restaurant seemed appropriate. Nearly soundlessly, she slipped out of her house to acquire her props.

Within forty-five minutes, Naomi was walking up the

driveway to Bethann's front door. A car in front of the garage door puzzled her a little. Oh, well, perhaps I am not the first to arrive. The Ring doorbell made a robotic sound unlike her own melodious chimes.

Naomi took a deep breath, preparing to ooze empathy. Instead, when the door opened, she sucked in an additional little gasp. "I, uh, you. Oh my." Recovering from her initial flustered response, "I am Naomi Khan von Hapsburg, and you absolutely must be Bethann's sister. The resemblance is remarkable!" In truth, the woman's appearance was as if Bethann had completed a wilderness nature hike and failed to collect her original demeanor.

Maryann smiled forgivingly and invited Naomi inside. The smell of sage drifted through the entryway. "I am smudging the house," Maryann explained. "Sadness has its own scent."

"I suppose," Naomi murmured, realizing she still held her token gestures. "Here, I thought you might need a bit of cheering up after learning about your sister." The flowers were accepted. "Oh, and no doubt you will want to have some quiet time off campus, as we say. The Hot Coals is only a few minutes away, and they offer a nice atmosphere."

As Maryann expressed her appreciation, Naomi's gaze drifted to the office alcove where she noticed two people leaning over the desk. "You already have company!"

Mildred and Ed barely glanced up from the laptop. "These kind folks are helping me straighten out some business and deal with the authorities."

"Authorities?"

"You know, paperwork as the heir and," Maryann shuddered. "The coroner, too," she added.

"Well, those two are certainly into details," Naomi said, keeping her face composed as she wondered what details they might discover.

"Everyone has been so kind. Tonight, I am meeting a neighbor for dinner."

Naomi had her suspicions about who that neighbor was but gently bit her tongue. "I will leave you three here to sort through estate details. Again, so sorry for your loss." Naomi turned towards the door, unwilling to announce that her soirée had been the last event Bethann attended.

Naomi stomped down the driveway. She clenched her teeth as the image of Ed and Mildred looking at the laptop swam in her memory. Her neighbor, 'the detective' had been 'on the scene' with Bethann. Even so, Naomi was more annoyed with Mildred's continued intrusion. She could almost re-taste the bitter facial she had worn on their last encounter.

Her march was interrupted by a text from Gunther.

He would not be home for dinner. He had a last-minute business meeting at the Lazy Lotus. Naomi narrowed her eyes and pictured the plush green velvet couches there. She visualized Gunther leaning into Maryann's personal space, offering a shoulder and more to the grieving sister who looked so much like his former lover.

The Medical Examiner

On the way over to pick up Maryann, Mil and I got a chance to cover something. "I've never dealt with or even met the Scotts County Medical Examiner. We know what we want..."

"Sure, Ed. An autopsy and toxicology exam."

"Our problem is overcoming that initial presumption when anybody in our age group..."

Mil cleared her throat.

"Okay, when anyone in my age group dies."

"Correction noted." Mil smiled wide.

"It's almost always believed to be natural causes. The body just wore out. And all we have to offer are our unofficial suspicions." I paused. "Here's the thing. I have no idea how political this ME's office is. The Sheriff is running for reelection. Going into the election, he certainly wouldn't want an unsolved murder on the books."

"Bethann's sister making the request might do it."

"Here's hoping." I sighed. "We'll play everything else close to the vest."

When we pulled into the drive, Maryann walked out the front door. "My God," I said, "she really does look like her sister."

"It is the clothing. She dressed out of the closet. Washed out her hair." Mil moved her eyes down. "Look, she's wearing real shoes."

"I think," I said, "there's actual make-up." I hopped out of the car and opened the back door for Maryann.

"Do you mind sitting in the back?"

"That's fine." She slid in, smoothed her skirt down and buckled up. Her tattoos were covered; her outfit offered a modest but noticeable bit of cleavage. She met my eyes. "I thought this might help."

"Never hurts," I said. "You look fine."

"Fine? You look great." Mil turned her head and spoke across the seat. "It is so nice that you and your sister are the same size."

"Shoes and everything. What are the odds?" Maryann dropped her voice. "But this brassiere, it is a torture device. I haven't worn one for years. When did they start putting metal wires in them?"

"When they ran out of whalebone, I guess." I buckled

in, waiting for a laugh. Mil and Maryann looked at me with disdain.

"Men," they said, almost able to keep a straight face, before laughing out loud.

As we drove, Mil ran through what would probably happen at the ME's. "Usually," she said, "the body is covered with a sheet except for the head. We may be in a viewing room looking through glass, or we may be led into a private room beside the gurney."

Maryann nodded. "I've been through this before. Years ago. My husband, my late husband...a climbing accident in New Mexico." She paused, took a deep breath. "The person you knew, the one who made you love and laugh, they are long gone. Their soul is out, waiting to be reborn. What's left is an empty vessel, their last earthly vestige." We were quiet for a while after that.

The outside landscape had the markings of autumn, browning grass, flame red and soft yellow leaves still hanging on, stem by stem, hopeful of extending their life.

Maryann spoke up from the back seat. "There's something you two should know. The reason I wanted to see the bathroom, the house, where she died...I've been there before."

"Maryann, I thought," Mil said, "I mean, you told us you had never been in Trivolity before."

133

"That's true."

"So how..." I started.

"She died on the night of the waning gibbous moon, right?"

"Okay," I said, having no idea. "The waning gibbous moon." Mil looked at me, just as baffled.

Maryann said, "You two don't know the phases of the moon and their significance? They don't teach that in your investigation courses?"

"They don't," Mil agreed. "Well, not at the FBI academy."

"The night of the waning gibbous moon is a time of self-reflection and letting go. It is a time to reset your soul. That night, I was in the stone garden at the ashram, meditating. And while deep into the universal mind, I had a vision." She closed her eyes and continued. "I saw my sister ascend a staircase, the same staircase we walked up in that house you took me to visit. Down below there was a sea of people, drinking, laughing; it was a party."

She paused, opened her eyes, then continued. "This is going to sound weird, but all the men looked like Abraham Lincoln, solemn, bearded, and wearing dark stovepipe hats. And the, well, the women were all dressed as if they were in Marie Antoinette's court, rouge-heavy faces, lace gowns, and curled wigs. I think they were waving goodbye to her on the stairs. She was waving back, that royal wave where you keep your hand locked, fingers together." She demonstrated.

"Got it," I said. "Like the Queen of England out with her corgis for a Sunday carriage ride."

"Exactly." After a sigh, Maryann continued. "Maybe waving, I don't know for sure. These visions are not an exact science."

"Sure," I said, not at all sure. "I get that."

"I was at the party," Mil said, "dressed a little different."

"I mean, I'm sure they were not actually dressed like that, I'm sure. Where would you even get that many top hats? But in this vision...anyway." She paused. "Next, I saw my sister, reflected in that ornately framed bathroom mirror, holding a cup or glass up to her mouth. The contents had a color to it, maybe a dark shade of blue-green? Then, just as suddenly, she was sprawled on the floor, reaching for her phone." She paused again, drew in a deep breath. "And then there was nothing left to see. She was gone." Neither Mil nor I said anything. "It was the same mirror, the same bathroom where she died. That's why," Maryann said, "I believe you two. Someone killed her. That's why we need an autopsy."

The Medical Examiner's Office was in a relatively new,

large red brick government building in the center of Scottsville, the county seat. It shared the three-story, low-slung building with other medical services, including the EMS and a counseling service. The offices had a clean, efficient, and modern look.

We were met promptly at the reception desk by a white coated woman, her face vaguely East Asian. "I'm Dr. Helen Watkins, one of the ME's, that is Medical Examiners, here." We introduced ourselves, and one by one, she offered her hand. Dr. Watkins led us through a mock mahogany door into another waiting room. "Would you prefer to make the identification through a viewing glass, or would you rather be in the same room?"

"If I could be nearer to the body," Maryann said.

"Of course. Please follow me." We did.

The room was cold, plain, and almost generic. It smelled faintly of cleaning products beneath a weak lemon scent.

Bethann was on a gurney, her head visible, the body, her body, covered by a white sheet. There were slight bruising and an abrasion around her right temple. It was the first time I saw her without make-up. The vibrant Bethann I knew, had known, somehow looked younger, naked and vulnerable.

"That's my sister," Maryann said, her voice caught.

"Bethann."

"We'll note the positive ID," Dr. Watkins said. "Thank you for coming in."

"Please, can I touch her," Maryann asked, "her body?"

"Of course."

Maryann reached below the sheet, lightly touching her sister's hand, and bowed her head. She was silent, her eyes closed, but her lips moved. It was less than a minute, she squeezed the hand, looked up, and said, "Thank you."

"Now if there's nothing else..." Dr. Watkins turned toward the door.

"I want an autopsy," Maryann said in a soft voice. "I want you to perform an autopsy."

We stood by while Maryann filled out the appropriate forms. Bethann remained nearby, her face expressionless. The ME requested, via cell phone, that an assistant bring out the last effects gathered at the scene.

"Dr. Watkins," I said, "can my associate and I speak with you for a moment? Perhaps best in private."

"Certainly." A young man entered the room, a plastic bag in his hand. You could see the clothing Bethann had been wearing through the clear plastic. She said to the young man, "Tom, this is the sister of the deceased. Can you help her complete the forms and return the effects to her?"

"Yes, Doctor," the clerk said.

"We'll be right back," Dr. Watkins said, already leading us out the door.

I explained to the ME, our professional backgrounds and our suspicions of foul play. She raised an eyebrow at the mention of my time in CPD Homicide and Mil's in the FBI.

"We're here on behalf of Maryann, the decedent's sister. She hired me, in my role as a North Carolina Licensed Private Investigator," I pulled my laminated license card from my pocket and offered it to her, "and my associate is working for me under that license."

Dr. Watkins examined my card, pulled out a pen, wrote down my name and the license number. "You know I'll have to notify the Sheriff's Department."

"I'm aware. We intend on speaking to the Sheriff when you discover it is a homicide."

"If," Dr. Watkins said.

I nodded, "If."

I pulled out the plastic bag containing the Q-tip swab. "When I found Bethann on the floor, without a pulse, I noticed a greenish material in the corner of her mouth. I used this swab to collect it. If she was poisoned, this may test positive for that poison."

"Did she have any medical conditions which either of you were aware of?"

"She was a diabetic," Mil said. "Based on the daily supply we found in her refrigerator," Mil held up a picture on the screen of her phone, "she had already taken her daily treatment."

"Please forward me that picture and any pictures that show the deceased as you found her."

"Of course," I said. "We will cooperate in any way we can."

Dr. Watkins continued, "You know, this is not an inexpensive procedure. Especially including a full toxicology spectrum. If nothing suspicious turns up, your client may be on the hook for the cost."

"We think that's unlikely. Our professional experience has led us to believe foul play was involved," I said. "And my client is aware of the financial consequences if..."

"I can assure you," Dr. Watkins said, "I and my department will do our best."

"That's all we ask," Mil replied. Dr. Watkins led us back to Maryann and the clerk. Maryann was still seated at a small desk while the assistant stood nearby.

"All finished," Tom said, holding up some papers. "I'll

go make some copies."

Dr. Watkins said, "Why don't you wait in the reception area, we'll bring the copies to you."

Handshakes were exchanged. Maryann remained quiet, almost appearing to nap on her feet, through the whole proceeding.

Waiting for us in the reception area was a khaki-clad, red in the face, sheriff's deputy. "There you are! Tom called me about you. You are the two," his voice was sharp and loud, "who're wasting this woman's money!" He had close-cropped dirty straw hair and an overly muscled frame, muscles that may have been helped along by steroid use. The active adult acne visible on the back of his neck as he turned lent credence to a juicing theory. The acne, along with the out-of-proportion anger.

Maryann drew herself up straighter. "My sister's dead. No one is wasting anything except you; you're wasting my time."

"Maryann," Mil said, "why don't you sit down over there?" She pointed to a long, padded bench along the wall, "while we talk to this," Mil's voice got a little louder, "fine representative of local law enforcement." Maryann made her way over to the bench and glared at the Deputy.

"And you are?" I said.

"I am Scotts County Deputy Sheriff Tyron Barbee, and I hate to see this poor woman be taken advantage of in her hour of grief." He delivered his little speech like he had been drawn out of the audience and onto the stage during amateur night at the improv.

"Deputy, I assure you, no one is taking advantage of anyone." I continued. "We are representing this woman while we try to determine exactly what happened."

He dropped his voice, "Don't be trying to bullshit me. You two know what happened. An old woman died. Old people die every day in that place, hell, all around here. You live, you get old, you die. Plain and simple."

Mil said, "It wasn't that simple."

"Listen lady, I was there! I saw the body. I made the call."

"Wait," I said, "you were there?"

Mil said, "Where exactly?"

"I'm the one asking questions here," Deputy Sheriff Barbee said.

"Mr. Barbee," Mil said, "I was at the party, and you were most definitely not in attendance."

"That's Deputy Sheriff Barbee," he said.

"Deputy, I was the person who discovered the body. I

did not see any representative from the Scotts County Sheriff's Department."

Deputy Sheriff Barbee shifted from foot to foot. "I was there."

"You definitely were not in the house," Mil said.

"And definitely not in the bathroom." I added, "I stayed upstairs until the EMTs moved the body."

"And I watched them move the body down the stairs and through the doors," said Mil.

"I was there," he said, his voice in a petulant tone.

"I can ID the EMTs if needed." Mil continued. "We can ask them where you were. Their offices are in this complex, right?"

"I stayed outside to control the scene," the deputy said.

"So, to summarize," Mil said, "you were there but not at the crime scene, not with the body as it was discovered upstairs. You examined the body..."

The deputy shifted his feet. "I saw her on the gurney."

"You pulled back the covering? Examined the body in the driveway?" Mil waited.

"I saw her head, her face."

"And that extensive exam of her head led you to believe she died of natural causes?" Mil paused. "And of course you noted the wound on her forehead?"

"Look, I don't want to talk about this anymore. She

died of natural causes. Even the EMTs thought so."

"Well, deputy, the ME is going to take a look, and I guess we will see," I said, offering my hand.

Deputy Barbee looked down, snorted, and said, "You two clowns are looking for a payday. You're not fooling me." He spun and started toward the door.

"We will be reading your site report," Mil said, loud enough for his departing figure to hear, "with interest, Deputy." The door shut.

Mil motioned to Maryann, who joined us and said, "Well, he seemed pleasant."

As we left the facility we saw, there in the parking lot, Deputy Barbee, phone out, taking pictures of our car and license plate.

As we went forward, he scurried away.

"I hope he got a nice, clear picture of my North Carolina Sheriff's Association honorary membership sticker," I said, chuckling.

"What's so funny?" Mil asked.

"I was just thinking of that aura thing you were telling us about, Maryann. Did Deputy Barbee have an aura? What did it tell you about him?"

"His aura was dark, black, and red and bits of orange, all swirling. Angry, unsettled, unhappy, and impulsive."

"That certainly sounds like him," I said.

"And there was a big blank break in the middle, where it isn't blending with the universe," Maryann continued. "I've been told those blank spaces may be filled in by inflicting damage on others." She paused. "By harming someone, you can steal parts of their energy and fill in those blank spaces."

"You don't say."

"But isn't it also true that those blank spaces may be filled by inflicting good on others?" Mil asked.

"You are correct, Mil. Good always outweighs the bad."

"I still don't get it," I said. "What exactly are auras?"

"Simply put, it's a reflection of energy surrounding all living things. In humans, especially, that energy is reflected in colors which give us clues to their life, emotions, and their spiritual resources. Different colors mean different things."

"Huh," I said. "How come you can read them, and I can't?"

"I can't tell you that. I was born this way. I just assumed everyone else saw auras too until I kept getting teased and treated like I was a freak. Growing up, I felt as if my gift was more like a curse."

"Okay, tell me about our auras." I gestured to myself and Mil.

"Come on, Ed. Leave Maryann alone. Enough with the aura questions."

"It's okay, Mil. I got this. You two are very similar. That's why I trusted you both from the beginning. You are both nicely blended across the spectrum, no one color dominating. Harmony reigns."

"You met Gunther. What's your read on him?"

"He's unlikable, a conniving user. I can't believe Bethann was involved with him."

"I think Ed meant his..." Mil seemed almost embarrassed to ask, "his aura."

"Oh, yes. Gunther has a lot in common with the deputy. Lots of black, red and orange. Swirling, shooting off like flares. And some blank spaces."

I wasn't quite sure what to say. "That seems telling."

"It is," Maryann said quietly, "not something to be ignored."

We rode most of the way back in silence. Before we pulled in through the gates, Maryann said, "Can I ask a favor?"

"Sure," I said.

"My supply of medicine is running really, really,

desperately low. Is there any place around here where I could re-up my herbal needs?"

"Well, marijuana above a certain dose is not legal in North Carolina," I told her.

"Except at an Indian, that is, Native American dispensary," Mil said. "And that one is two and a half hours away, over near the mountains."

"Near a casino, I think. But," I said, "there are vape and herb shops around here that sell legal levels, Delta 8 and 9."

"You seem like you know about this stuff," Mil said.

"My knees. I'm on meds for my arthritis, my knees, left hip, big toes, and hands. But sometimes I need a little help, beyond Advil and Aleve. My wife said, 'Hey, we're retired, no one cares, give it a try.'"

Mil said, "And it helps?"

"It helps."

"So, just like the children's song," Mil said.

"Huh?" I asked.

"Heads, shoulders, knees, and toes," Mil sang.

From the back seat, Maryann sang, "Knees and toes, knees and toes." They both started laughing.

We dropped Mil off and drove out along route 73. "Where you hit business 16, there's a strip mall coffee shop, cake shop, nail and hair salons, and a weed store,"

Ed said. "Get your gummies, cure your munchies, maybe get that streak of purple in your hair, all at one stop." He laughed.

Once inside, Maryann explored all the under-glass displayed products. At one point, she turned to me and said, "This is like taking baby aspirin to cure a sucking chest wound. Or applying a tincture of Mercurochrome to a severed limb."

"I get the overly graphic picture, but until we can get you to Cherokee, try to make the best out of..."

'Yeah, yeah," she said, flicking her fingers at me.

Getting the clerk over to a display case, she pointed and asked a bunch of technical questions. After some discussion, she selected and purchased multiple items, gummies, tinctures, and vapes.

Once in the car, Maryann ripped open a foil pack of Orange-Mango Kush and stuffed a gummy into her mouth. She offered me the foil pack.

"Thanks, but no," I said. "I'm driving."

"Your loss," she said, grabbing another one and stuffing it into her mouth.

She chewed one more on our way to her house.

Three Part Harmony

Gunther heard the muffled sounds of Naomi stirring as he sipped his morning cappuccino. The cognac added just the perfect balance to smooth out the morning ritual to come. He had slept well in the main-floor bedroom, accompanied by many blissful dreams of Maryann.

Oh, what a pleasant surprise it had been when she had arrived at his front door the other day. Such an uncanny resemblance to Bethann! Finally, to meet Maryann, the person from the texts. And she is Bethann's sister! My dream of gaining the mineral rights may yet come true! And the exquisite quiver at my touch as she left confirms the electric connection between us.

Lunch today at the Lazy Lotus will be the perfect opportunity to advance our relationship. Much better than meeting for dinner, fewer prying eyes. All the better to practice my charms and win her!

More sounds from upstairs brought him back to the cappuccino and his current reality. The tigress was emerging from her lair, he thought. If it's Tuesday, then it's Pilates with Eric. All the women at Trivolity were quite taken by him. But Naomi had staked her claim. The fresh young meat was hers. Well, it's good she has a hobby; it gets her out of the house.

As she came into the kitchen, he was reminded of why he had married her all those years ago. Beauty and brains, not your usual trophy wife. She looked perfectly gorgeous, attired for her rendezvous, or, rather, Pilates class. "Good morning, Gunther. Enjoying your morning boozy coffee, I see."

"Yes, my love. Time was, you would have joined me. I see you have other plans."

She smiled and bestowed an air kiss, so as to not mess up her makeup. He remembered now why he wanted to leave her. It had always been the type of marriage necessary to maintain his status, and had been an equal partnership, yet never a loving one. Not like the excitement with sweet, departed Bethann.

Thank God, Bethann has a replacement. Gunther happily tapped one of his velvet house slippers on the upgraded Carrera marble floor. Maryann was a little too hippie-dippie for his taste, but she would do. He was now back to the same old conundrum: what to do about Naomi? She would never leave him. He couldn't leave her either; the prenup was ironclad. Back to the original plan, then.

"I am sure you have other activities today as well, dear heart," Naomi replied. "Don't forget your 'medication'. You wouldn't want anything to go wrong. Remember, we are meeting the Olsons for dinner at the Forge tonight," Naomi said on her way out.

Peacefully alone again, Gunther considered his options. Poisoning Naomi's mouthwash had not worked out well. Maybe her secret vodka stash? Yes, after *exercising with Eric*, Naomi does so enjoy a nice vodka and tonic while soaking in our hot tub.

He began to play the scene out. Sadly, on my return home, I will discover, to my horror, that she drifted off and drowned. My new status as a bereaved husband will only enhance my already significant appeal to the fairer sex of the community. Maryann and I will surely commune over our recent losses, creating a bond.

Smiling, he retrieved the vial from his office safe. No half-measures this time, he told himself. He decanted the whole vial into the vodka bottle.

That should do it. I'll be out with Maryann when she returns. Those keystone cop detectives won't suspect a thing. Time to prepare for our date. Which cologne should I splash on? What are the young kids wearing these days? Hatchet? No, ah, Axe, that's it. Ready or not, Maryann, here I come.

###

This is the strangest place, Maryann thought, as she pulled up to the Lazy Lotus in the VW Microbus she had rented at the airport. She never understood why Bethann would want to live in such a cookie-cutter community. Sure, there were some beautiful sunsets, but I had plenty of those in New Mexico. And the vibe here! It was so uncool. Just a few minutes talking with the investigators, and it was pretty clear: there were so many secrets.

Ed and Mildred were wonderful people, so I guess I shouldn't let a few bad apples ruin the bunch. Mil especially seemed to groove on the sense of community. Who'd have thought I would like an ex-Fed? These days, it's hard to know who the bad guys are.

Mil filled her in on Gunther, the creepy dude who touched her when they first met. Who does that? Right, creepy dudes. When she told Ed about Sir Handsalot, he said, 'Good! We need to know more about him and Bethann. I don't think he did it, but get close to him—not too close, of course. He may know something'. So, now I'm a

151

narc. Definitely uncool. The things I do for a sister.

Maryann sighed, got out of the minibus, and walked up to the restaurant. Another dull storefront with assorted kitschy decorations. No Georgia O'Keeffe's here, she thought as she entered.

"Hi there," the hostess greeted her, smiling. "Welcome to the Lazy Lotus, where the service is our good name. Do you have a reservation?"

Maryann surveyed the restaurant, trying to see if Gunther had already arrived. He wasn't at the bar, and the rest of the dining room was composed of darkened, private booths. I see why he picked the place, she realized. A private place where no one from Trivolity would see them. What happens at the Lazy Lotus stays at the Lazy Lotus.

"No, I'm meeting someone here, Gunther von Hapsburg."

"Oh, yes," replied the hostess. She took another look at Maryann. "I'm sorry, I didn't recognize you, Ms. Cook."

"You mean, my sister, Bethann. Did she dine here often?"

"Yes, she and Mr. von Hapsburg dined here often. I will take you to him. This way, please." A little confused over all the Ann names, the hostess turned with a frown.

She led Maryann to a booth in the back, where she found Gunther nursing a cocktail. He was smartly dressed, complete with an Ascot. It's like he thinks he's Fred Astaire or something. Give me a guy in jeans and a T-shirt, any day.

He smiled and said, "Hello, Maryann. It is so nice to see you again!"

As she slid into the booth, she detected a strong, odd smell. They must have cleaned the booth with Lysol or something, she thought. Poor Gunther, they must have used a lot on his side of the booth. He reached out his hand, palm up, as if he were assisting her to the table. She smiled and sat down.

"Can I get you a drink?" he asked.

"Sure, any kind of THC seltzer would be fine. Pomegranate, if they have it."

"Sorry," said Gunther, his eyebrows arching in confusion. "Do you mean vodka seltzer?"

"No, not that. You know THC. Cannabis, they must have that here."

"My dear, that's illegal in this state," he said. Gunther took hold of his napkin, unfolding it and placing it on his lap.

"Oh, that's right, I forgot. Force of habit. Fine, then I'll have a Poison Kiss Martini."

"Poison?" said Gunther. "Poison Kiss?"

"You know, vodka, vermouth, some Tabasco. Don't worry, I'm sure they know how to make one." Why's he asking about that, she wondered. It's not like I'm asking him to mix one up for me. Maryann noticed a change in Gunther's aura, yellow creeping in, taking over. Was it something I said? Or maybe my resemblance to Bethann? "It's still hard to think of Bethann in the past tense," Maryann said. "I know you were good friends. She talked about you a lot." Not really, Maryann thought, but Mil said that would be a good way to get him talking.

"Poison Kiss Martini," Gunther said, his voice shaking. "Why would anyone name a drink that? Alcohol isn't poison, is it?"

It appears I've derailed Gunther. I wonder what I said? It's no telling just how little it takes for these 'elderly people' to get hung up on some triviality, thought Maryann.

"Maybe it is. Maybe it is poison," he continued. His hand shook as he glanced at his watch. "Oh. Look at the time! I forgot; I have another appointment. I must be on my way. Let's do this again." Apologizing, he stood up, extracted himself from the booth and headed quickly for the door.

Well, damn, she thought, that was abrupt. What has him so jumpy? Mentally, she went back over their conversation. The only thing that came to mind was when his aura spiked. It was when she asked for the Poison Kiss Martini. Hmm. Poison. There must be something there. But what?

"Pardon me," the server interrupted her thoughts. "May I get you anything else?"

"Oh, no thank you, I'm good."

"OK, I'll be back with the check."

Great, Gunther stiffed me with the check. That's harsh.

What have I done? Gunther thought as he raced his car down Business 16. Slow down! he told himself. You don't want a ticket, not now. You don't need to bring suspicion on yourself.

Why did Maryann order that drink? With that name, Poison Kiss Martini? Does she know? Do they know? Calm down! You almost ran the red light, the voice in his head reprimanded. The poison was supposed to be undetectable. That's what Troy said. "Undetectable!" Somewhere, well ahead of him, sirens wailed. His heart started pounding. There's always someone needing an ambulance at Trivolity, or maybe just another golf cart fire.

What if someone found Naomi dead, poisoned? Don't think it! A man of substance does not panic! Just get home and get rid of the bottle, the evidence, that is. Finally, Gunther reached the gate and slowed down to the residential limit. The sirens had stopped, but they always shut them down once inside the community proper. He drove on to his street, Blow Hard Circle, swerving wildly to avoid someone walking in the street. Why do they never use the sidewalk?

Damn, they're at my house! And Naomi's car is there. Wait, she's getting out of the car. She's OK. He had a sinking feeling. Maybe a smoke detector, then? He slowed down and parked on the street behind another car. It had 'Carol Maid For You' stenciled on the side. Probably at the neighbor's, we're not due yet.

Then he heard the familiar anguished cry that could only come from Naomi, "Dear sweet Mother of God, not again! Not in my house! What is wrong with these people?" she wailed.

Gunther hesitated by his car, debating whether to avoid the storm or face it head-on. At least, it's nothing I did, he thought. Head on, then. But what happened? He continued on to the house and entered.

The body on the floor looked vaguely familiar. Was it Carol? One can never keep the hired help straight. But that's next week, isn't it?

"Why does this keep happening to us?" he heard Naomi lament. "Just look at that mess! There's blood on my Carrara marble floor. And now who's going to clean it? Tell me who? Good cleaners are so hard to find. Why must we always be the ones suffering?"

Gunther looked past the EMT's and saw the vodka bottle on the kitchen counter. "I don't understand. Who found her?"

The EMT answered, "We got a 911 call, the door was unlocked, and we found her lying on the floor. It seems she hit her head on the island. She was dead before we got here."

"But how?" asked Gunther.

"Gunther! What happened?" asked someone behind him. He whirled around in the direction of the voice and saw Ed Prescott at the front door, wearing a Cleveland police department sweatshirt and shorts. Gunther hung his head. 'Can it get any worse?' he wondered.

"I just finished my walk, and I saw the EMS truck," said Ed. He leaned into the room, taking his phone out. He walked up to the body and began talking to the tech, while he knelt to examine the body. Gunther took the opportunity to edge his way over to the vodka bottle in the kitchen. A sizable amount was missing. He had heard rumors about Carol. It's too late to lock the drinks cabinet now, he thought. While Prescott was busy, Gunther quietly stowed the bottle in a cupboard under the counter.

As he turned back to the body, he saw the EMT help Ed up. He was sweaty from his walk. Naomi glared at the detective but appeared resigned to having her house once again overrun by unwelcome guests.

"Sorry," said Ed. "I'm worn out from that walk. Mind if I sit down?" Gunther saw the horror on his wife's face as Ed collapsed in her favorite chair. The detective looked from Gunther to Naomi and said, "One death in your house may be regarded as unfortunate; two looks like carelessness."

Suspicion Mounts

"Something's not right at the von Hapsburgs," Mil said, as she clicked open her briefcase and removed her accumulated notes. "Last week, I'd swear Gunther had nothing to do with the murder, but now, with another death happening under the same roof, I'm not so sure."

"I've been thinking the same thing," Ed said. "It's too much of a coincidence. We need to take a second look."

"Well, at least we know one thing," Mil said, snickering as she watched Ed return Gunther's picture to the Murder Board.

"What's that?" Ed asked.

"Our murderer is definitely not a professional!"

"What makes you say that, Mil?" he asked, the beginning of a smile tugging at his mouth.

"Because no self-respecting professional killer would strike twice under the same roof, barely a week apart.

They'd have to be really stupid to do that."

Ed nodded. "Agreed. But so far, Bethann's death has been attributed to natural causes. You and I just happen to not believe that." Ed tapped the end of his pencil against his lips. "There's another possibility. If Carol's death was not an accidental fall, then, we could have two murderers on our hands!"

"Hmm! I hadn't thought of that." Mil spread the crime scene photos from the maid's murder out on Ed's desktop as she continued talking. "Let's go back to Gunther. What motive would he have to commit these murders?"

"Jealousy. Maybe he was having an affair with Bethann and didn't like her flirting with others, or maybe Naomi found out, and she decided to take care of it herself. You know, the whole 'He's my man' thing."

Mil shook her head. "Naomi is bitchy enough, but I don't see her doing it, especially in her own boudoir. And Gunther seems too narcissistic to want to spoil his party with anything so sinister. But still, he's definitely hiding something."

"What about the conversation you overheard at The Forge?" Ed said. "Something about Gunther and the land the community is built on? Maybe there's something there."

"Could be, but right now, the only fact connecting the

two murders is the location."

Mil pulled a chair up to Ed's side of the desk. "Let's look at the pictures. Hopefully, between the two of us something will jump out."

For the next several minutes, only the faint rustle of printed paper, and an occasional sniffle, could be heard as side-by-side Mil and Ed examined the pictures on the desk. After a while, Ed got out the magnifying glass to take an even closer look. Lately, close work really strained his injured eye.

Meanwhile, Mil said, "I need to take a break. My back's killing me." She stood and stretched side to side before moving toward the window.

"Go ahead," Ed said. "I'll do the same in a minute. Something about this picture bugs me. I—"

"Holy cow! Ed, come here. You've got to see this! It's the von Hapsburgs."

Ed jumped up and peered through the blinds, following Mil's gaze across the street to the open garage. "Looks like they're arguing."

"I'd say." They watched Naomi flailing her arms and stomping her feet. "I wish we could hear what they're saying."

"Maybe this will help." Ed slowly lifted the blinds and cracked the window. Together they leaned closer to the screen.

Mil shook her head. "Definitely shouting going on over there but I can't make out what they're saying. Oh look! She's pointing at the trash cans and shaking her head. Now her hands are in the air and she's backing up. Seriously? Could they be arguing about who's moving them out to the curb? Can you make out what they're saying?"

"No. It could be about the trash. Tomorrow is pickup day. Come to think of it, I've never seen them put the trash out before. It's always been—"

"The maid," Mil and Ed said together. A few minutes elapsed until the sound of rolling wheels drew their attention back to the window.

"Oh my God!" Ed said, trying to hold in laughter. "Look at Gunther!"

"What the heck is he wearing? A mask? Is that a raincoat? And look at the pink rubber gloves pulled up to his elbows." Mil worked to contain her laughter. Ed couldn't contain his. He burst out in hysterical laughter as Gina entered the room with a bowl of chips and two cold beers.

"What's going on? I thought you were working?" she said as she set the snacks on the file cabinet.

He waved her over to the window. "You gotta see

this!"

"Now Ed," Gina said, moving toward the window, "it's not polite to spy on our neigh...Oh my God! Am I seeing what I think I'm seeing?"

The distinct clink of glass in the recycle bin carried toward Ed's window as it bumped to the curb.

Gina laughed. "Now that beats everything."

"We figured that normally was the maid's job," Mil said.

"Oh, the poor woman. The von Hapsburgs couldn't have been easy to work for and then to die in the process. It's tragic. Just tragic. Are you any closer to solving it?" Gina asked in a sympathetic tone.

"We're working on it. Something's got to give soon," Ed said. "Thanks for the snacks. We'll just be another hour or so," he told his wife. The investigators returned to the pictures on the desk.

"Let's try something different," Mil suggested. "Let's lay the photos out in order, and compare them that way."

"Okay," Ed said. "Here are two of the area where the body was found."

Mil leaned over. "Nothing different in them. Agreed?"

"Agreed!" Ed put those aside and shuffled through the photos.

She picked one up that matched two he had just

found. "Here are three similar shots with the body in place." Together they studied them side-by-side.

Suddenly Ed said, "Wait! Look closely, Mil. What do you see, or rather don't see?"

She stared, squinting, and started to shake her head, and then she saw it. On the counter, above where the body lay, were liquor bottles. Six in two photos and only five in the ones taken later. "One bottle is missing," Mil said. "The fancy odd shaped one in black!"

They both looked at each other and at the same time said, "Trash!" Back at the window, they looked out at the von Hapsburg's trash cans on the curb.

"We have to go through their trash!" Ed said.

"My thinking exactly!" Mil said. "What's our plan?"

"Pickup is in the early morning. I'll go out around midnight when most are in bed and switch bins."

"What if you're caught?"

"I won't be. No one's around at midnight on a weekday. Besides, If I am, I'll think of something. I learned a thing or two working for years with liars and thieves." Ed said, laughing. He walked with her to the front door and opened it for her.

"Call me if you find the fancy black bottle. Goodnight. Nice work today. Looks like we may finally have a breakthrough, at least for the maid's murder."

Ed waved to Mil as she left and took one last look across the street before going inside.

"Are you coming to bed anytime soon?" Gina secured the belt to her terrycloth robe around her waist as she leaned into Ed's office. "You've been working on the case ever since Mil left. Time to give it a rest."

"I will, dear. Almost done," Ed punched one final thing into his computer, turned off the light, and stood up. He stopped at the window for a last look across the street. Everything was clothed in darkness, except for a single streetlamp swaying in the wind, its motion bathing the sidewalk several houses down in undulating shadows. Spooky, Ed thought. Passing Gina in the hallway, Ed said, "I'll be back in a minute. I forgot to put the trash cans out."

"Okay, dear," Gina said. "I'm going to bed."

Ed made his way to the side of the house and, slowly, to keep the noise down, rolled his recycle bin to the street. Stopping to listen, he looked around. Not a soul was about. His heart beat wildly as he pulled the bin across the concrete to the von Hapsburg's driveway. Suddenly, an owl screeched. Ed stifled a cry and ducked down behind the bin, breathing heavily. He waited for what seemed like minutes, then slowly stood up. Quickly, he made the switch. No one appeared to be awake to witness the deed.

Back in his own garage after calming down, Ed donned non-pink rubber gloves, opened the von Hapsburg's bin, and shined a miniature flashlight inside. Near the top, under empty bottles of The Forge's finest wines, a gold label on a black vodka bottle caught the light. The comparison between the bottle in the crime scene photo and the one laying in the trash bin looked like a match. Carefully, Ed picked it up and deposited it into a plastic bag. It would go to the lab in the morning for analysis.

The Treehouse Guy

Billy Dan peered skyward through the trees as the sun continued sinking below the horizon. Would tonight bring rain, or did the accumulating clouds simply provide the canvas for another gorgeous North Carolina sunset as the burning orb slipped below the horizon? He pulled his all-weather coat tighter around his middle and decided to chance an evening walk. BD, as his sisters Maryann and Bethann (rest her soul) called him, was uneasy tonight. He patted his pockets and glanced around the good-sized wooden platform secured in an ancient hickory tree, ensuring his few possessions were locked in the footlocker, before making his way down the sturdy wood and rope ladder to the ground. While two, three and even four-bedroom houses continued to sprout like invasive foreign plants all across the land where he'd been raised, Billy Dan chose to live in the only legacy structure that remained as per the contract with the builders: his childhood tree house.

The sisters' older brother had been heart broken when the land was sold. His many fond memories of growing up on the farm that once sat where the community now stood, urged him toward his leap of faith. He'd sold nearly all his possessions, purchased survivalist gear, and moved into the old tree house. The sale agreement had stipulated that the developers could not tear down the structure, and it was to be allowed to fall of its own accord. Billy Dan wasn't going to see that happen and spent many hours not only shoring up the structure but making improvements. For a tree house, it was now quite habitable.

Still, the eldest Cook sibling remained troubled. The only balm was walking, and so he walked. Miles and miles of trails that had been created from existing deer paths were his favorite routes, and when those were exhausted, he roamed the streets of Trivolity. He knew his appearance skewed toward wild, and to avoid being the source of dozens of phone calls to the HOA office, he traveled under darkness. The paths were well known to him, and it always pleased him to encounter the many creatures that most residents either didn't know existed or scared them silly. Coyotes, foxes, raccoons, opossums, deer, of course, and rumor had it, a bear, though Billy

Dan had never encountered one. He was of the mind that more than a few residents had overactive imaginations.

People who spent their lives swaddled in cities or suburbia suddenly thought themselves experts on wildlife. Now, living here, they encountered such savage creatures as lizards, snakes, and mice and had the idiocy to try either to chop the reptiles into bits, or poison the little furry things. So deep was their narcissism that they didn't realize that all of nature is connected. Snakes keep the rodent population at bay, and by killing snakes, rodents thrive. When the suddenly abundant mice are poisoned, birds of prey like hawks and owls die of the toxins in the mice they eat, too. Billy Dan sighed as he trudged along, remembering with sadness the tiny Saw Whet owl he found dead by the bridge on Expedition Boulevard. No doubt the victim of such egregious stupidity.

He continued along the trail that dropped further into the wooded area, heading for the section of creek nearest the quarry. On the creek's shore, he had once cleared a small patch of scrub grass and dumped a bucketful of sand for a miniature fire pit, ringing it with rocks. The evening was still fairly mild for this time of year, but chilly enough for a small blaze. It had been a good area for fishing at one time, and he remembered sneaking away from his chores on summer afternoons to catch a few brook trout. Now, as he coaxed fire from dry twigs and grass, his mind wandered to Bethann and her untimely demise. While he and Maryann were more alike in many ways, he and Bethann were close too, until they quarreled over her choice to purchase a house on their old homestead. He felt his continued presence on the land to be an act of protest, but that she had willingly given the developers her hard-earned money was a slap in the face.

An Eastern Screech Owl made itself heard as Billy Dan threw a foil-wrapped sweet potato into the coals to cook for his dinner. In the years he'd lived here, his way of life had shaved excess fat from his frame, and he was able to subsist on light fare. Every few months, he did consent to spend a night at Bethann's house, where he showered, ate a hearty meal, and slept in a real bed instead of the hammock he'd strung up in the treehouse. They reminisced about their childhood while she did his laundry, when she could talk him into it. Tension remained between them, however, and there were topics they agreed not to discuss.

He polished off the potato and stood up to stretch, thinking it was probably dark enough by now to continue his wanderings. He smothered the fire. Through the trees, a faint glow from the streetlights in the distance told him the evening was well underway. While there were private parties throughout the neighborhood any given night, for the most part, no one ventured out after the Club's closing hours. People returning home were too absorbed in trying to steer their vehicles to take much notice of a lone walker. That was why it took BD by surprise when he rounded a corner to see a man limping across the street, dragging his garbage bin behind him. Something struck him as odd, so he stepped behind the magnolia tree on the 'public' section near the corner and watched.

After scanning left and right down the street, the stranger reached for the bin on his neighbor's driveway and hauled that out into the street. Then, the man replaced it with the bin he'd brought with him. Glancing once more up and down the street, the garbage bin thief made his way back to his own side of the street. Instead of leaving the newly acquired bin on the driveway for collection, he continued with it into his garage. The sound of an automatic door engine hum, and an ear-piercing squeak of wheels on an unoiled track accompanied the door's drop. The street was quiet once again, though BD noticed fluorescent light streaming through the garage windows.

Deputized

"Mil," I said into the phone, a little breathless, "the ME called, results are in. She requested we meet her at the Sheriff's office tomorrow at 10:00. Does that work for you?"

"Sure, Ed," she said, "I can drive."

"Okay, see you at 9:15."

Mil's jeep was waiting at the end of the driveway as I walked out the door. The morning was a little cooler, our days hit the low eighties but overnight the temps dropped down to the upper sixties. Autumn was definitely here.

"Morning," I said as I climbed into the passenger side.

"Morning," Mil replied. She waited for me to buckle in, then drove down the drive and out of Trivolity, heading west on 73. The car radio was on. The Grateful Dead were singing about a 'Friend of the Devil'.

"I did not pick you as a Deadhead," I said.

Mil smiled. "I wasn't, my Dad was."

"The Army Colonel?"

Mil nodded. "He grew up in Southern California," she said. "Don't we all just listen to what we grew up with in our teens?"

"Sure," I said, knowing that my own ears expanded after High School.

"His career was the Army. I was an Army brat. The one thing I learned, here in America, in Germany, in Asia, no matter the post, someone was always playing the Dead. I guess it's my go to."

"It's just funny. When we dropped you off, after visiting the ME, Maryann asked if I would mind if she turned on the radio? 'Of course not,' I said. So, she turns on Sirius XM, and it's tuned to the Real Jazz station. 'I can't listen to jazz this early in the day,' she says. 'Have at it,' I say, 'anything you want.' So, she scans and browses until she hits on The Grateful Dead station."

"You're kidding."

"I kid you not. 'That's the one,' she said, and leaned back. We go into the store, she buys up half the stock, comes back into the car, starts munching gummies, and turns up the radio pretty loud. It was playing the same song."

"Weird." Mil laughed. "I listen to this station all the

time. Believe it or not, when doing cyber investigations, spending days in front of transactional codes on computer screens, you need something in your ears to keep your mind alert. For me," she paused, "it was the Dead. Sometimes Phish or some other jam band, but the Dead. Other squad members, heavy metal, classic rock, classical. Always the Dead for me."

"Well, this is where your fandom separates. So, Maryann tells me she followed the Dead tour around for a few months, selling candles and t-shirts and illegal substances, and, realizing what she just said, she stopped talking." I laughed. "You should have seen the look on her face. It was like she realized who she was talking to. Then Maryann continued on, like she was on the stand in court, 'Formerly illegal substances in the venue's parking lot to afford tickets and gas.' She did this from her late teens. Eventually found life in the ashram, used it as her base, and when the Dead came through the area, went out and followed them again. Did it off and on for 25 years."

"We were probably at the same concerts."

"Concerts?"

"You can't see them just once," Mil said.

"What did your fellow agents at the Bureau think?"

"You'd be surprised. There are Deadheads everywhere." Mil smiled, "Just breathing in at those concerts could be dangerous. You hoped that you weren't picked for a random drug screen in the next week. Then, you'd have some explaining to do."

###

The county seat of Scottsville, where the Sheriff's office was located, was only a half-hour or so away. There was barely any traffic. The surrounding trees had some fall colors, but if you looked closely, the browning grass and dry shrubs told of the needed rain.

"I'm thinking," I said, "we have a murder on our hands. The ME and, I suspect at the sheriff's direction, wouldn't ask us out here if it was a natural death."

"I had the same thought," Mil said.

"Have you met the Sheriff?"

"I've been thinking about that, maybe once, when I first moved in, at the retired agents' shoot."

I knew that when Bureau Agents retired, to keep themselves eligible for background check work or some other contract work, they participated in the local agency's firing range qualifications. This gave the retired agent a chance to establish connections with the branch and qualified them for most state's retired law enforcement status and concealed carry status. I attended retired officer shoots for the same reasons.

"I know the Sheriff a bit," I said. "He showed up at one of my shoots. Introduced himself, glad handed everyone. He's a real political creature. I ended up buying two tickets to his fundraising pig roast picnic. Gina and I showed up at the picnic, and he remembered my background and my name."

"Wow." She paused. "Is he competent?"

"Compared to the guy before. If you look through what's online, there are seventy deputies spread out through the detention center, patrol, and investigations. There's like one black guy in the command structure, and no women that I saw. And, I'm only saying this to give you a heads up, he supported the nutty guy who ran for Governor last time around..."

"The porn guy?"

"Yep. And I've seen pictures of him on stage at political rallies."

"I'm always circumspect," Mil said. "But, thanks for the heads up."

Meanwhile, in the background, the Dead warned, "Trouble ahead, there's trouble behind..."

###

We passed three or four bondsman companies offering their services. Each declaring on their face boards something like, 'We got the cash to set you FREE.' I knew we were close, detention centers are the bond's audience and customer base. Within two minutes, Mil pulled into the Sheriff's Department lot. Not surprisingly, the sheriff's department was housed in a building that looked a lot like the ME's building, red brick with off-white slate highlights, probably the same builder, probably at the same time. The big difference was the outside pen of the detention center, a fifteen-foot dual chain link fence topped by an inward facing three-foot section of razor wire. The inside ground was pacing worn grass. No one was out in the yard.

The sign above the entrance read:

HARVEN A. CROUSE
LAW ENFORCEMENT
AND DETENTION CENTER
OFFICE OF THE SHERIFF

Mil pulled a light jacket from the back seat and put it on, covering her sidearm. My own piece was in a concealed ankle holster. This time, we both carried notebooks.

"Ready?" Mil asked.

"Ready."

Sitting at a central desk in the lobby, the receptionist, a weary-looking woman, asked the nature of our visit, put a finger up and used the phone. "The Sheriff is expecting you, sign in," she pushed a clipboard forward and said, "wear these visitor badges," she placed two badges on the counter, "and a deputy will be down to escort you."

As we clipped the visitor badge on, a bright faced young man in a deputy's uniform came up to us and said, "Please follow me." When we walked down the long hall, the deputy moved with the cadence of a recent academy graduate, separating himself from us quickly. Looking back, he was gracious enough to wait for us to catch up and slowed his pace. We arrived at a door that bore the sheriff's badge and declared in capital letters OFFICE OF THE SCOTTS COUNTY NC SHERIFF. The deputy opened the door. Mil and I went in. The administrative assistant, who was much younger, prettier, and apparently less stressed, looked up from her computer screen, gave us a smile, and pointed to two chairs. The sheriff's actual office was behind another door. We sat and waited. Pictures of sheriffs, some past and current, adorned the walls.

We heard voices rising from the Sheriff's closed door office.

"Scotts County Deputy Sheriff Tyron Barbee," Mil whispered. I nodded.

Barbee said, in an angry voice, "I can't believe you're gonna let some pickleball retiree and a f-ing Fed DEI hire work on this. For all we know, they were involved."

In a loud, flat voice, the sheriff said, "Remember who you're talking to, deputy."

"Sheriff," Barbee said, "these Trivolity folks are living in homes built by illegal aliens, lawns cut by illegal aliens, probably some of them members of MS-13. What kinda judgment does that show?"

Mil whispered, "We have members of MS-13 cutting our lawns?" We both suppressed a laugh.

The volume of the discussion dropped. Minutes later, a red-faced Deputy Barbee came through the sheriff's office door, spotted Mil and me, and made a motion as if intending to slam the door shut. "Deputy," the sheriff commanded, "on your way out, leave the door open." Barbee raced from the room, out to the hall, snarling under his breath.

"The sheriff will see you now," the receptionist said in a cheerful voice.

###

The sheriff, seated behind his desk, stood up to greet us, walked around the furniture, and extended his hand. "Agent," he said to Mil, shaking her hand. "Ed," he said, his grip was firm and cool, "good to see you again. How's that lovely wife? Gina, right?"

"Yes, sir," I said, "good memory. Gina's well."

"Nice to hear, sit down, sit down." He indicated the two leather wing-backed chairs facing his desk. He returned to the desk. "The ME's here, but I wanted to run something by you. First, do you need water or coffee, or anything? No? Great." He opened a folder on his desk. "You've probably guessed that the ME has indeed found, as you two suspected, the death of Bethann...to be suspicious in nature. The toxicology report led us, well, the ME, to conclude poison was involved. Now it is the policy of this office to follow up on any suspicious deaths. Unfortunately, due to manpower shortages and prior commitments, if I kept this investigation in-house, it would become an inactive investigation. You both know what happens to inactive homicide investigations; leads grow cold, witnesses develop amnesia, details are lost." The sheriff paused as if expecting our reaction.

"That's my experience," Mil said.

"Yes, sir," I said. "In any suspicious death, time is of the essence."

"Exactly, I knew you two would get it. That's why I am going to propose a solution. Now I realize you're both working on this because an interested party..." he looked at the file.

"The victim's sister, sir," I said. "Maryann."

"Maryann and Bethann, huh? You sure the family doesn't have roots in one of the hollers down here?" He smiled at his joke. We smiled. "So you're already working on this under your PI License, right? How about we do this, since you two know the details so far. I mean, there wouldn't be any details without your work. How about you two work on this as newly appointed temporary deputies under my command?" Raising my eyebrows, I gave Mil a knowing glance, then turned back to the Sheriff. "You two can run the investigation, have access to our resources, databases, reports, what have you, and run this thing as you see fit."

"Well, sir, that is a generous offer," I said.

"Now I know both of you shoot; I've seen Ed myself, you both have private carry licenses. You can see my range officer if you want to make it official, but I'm good if you decide to just carry private. Less liability issues."

We stirred a bit, both realizing anything that would happen with our firearms, we'd be on our own, no implied immunity.

"But you'll get a badge, an identifying card, you can legally detain, refer charges, testify, and you can legally arrest. In addition, I can put you on a salary for the duration. We'll work the money details out. No vehicle, I'm afraid. I'll assign a liaison officer for anything you need from us, run players, background, whatever, you just have to go through this officer, Deputy Sheriff Helen Dewitt. She's a marvel. Could find a sand flea in a hurricane."

Mil asked, "If you don't mind, can we confer privately?"

"Sure, sure. Use my office. Let me just say, I hope you take the offer. Frankly, I do not have anybody on my team with your experience." He got up and left the office.

"What do you think?" said Mil.

"Sounds good. He doesn't want an open murder investigation in Trivolity during an election season. This is a way of keeping it quiet."

"The firearm thing is concerning."

"Agreed," I said. "But neither of us is going to use our weapon unless in self-defense or in defense of someone else. And under NC law, we'd be covered as private citizens."

"You're right," Mil said.

"Here's the other thing: one of the prior Sheriff's offices had a problem covering up information in a shooting incident."

"All right, I'm in."

I went to the door and opened it. "Sheriff," I said.

The sheriff walked in and sat on the front of his desk. "Before you say anything, Frannie, that is Miss Lewis, my secretary, er, administrative assistant, tells me you two were out there when I was dealing with a personnel problem. And you may have overheard certain remarks. I want to apologize, my employee said some things..."

"No offense taken," I said. Mil nodded.

"Look," the Sheriff said, "this guy is a loose cannon. He's not a bad person, heck, he's my wife's sister's son. I mean, we all have nephews, right? Be assured, I read him the riot act, and he will steer clear of any investigation. So, have you reached any decision?"

"Yes, we're agreed. We'd like to work the case," Mil said.

"Great, great, thank you both." He got off his desk, opened a drawer, pulled out two badges and ID cards, handing them over. "Now, if you'd raise your right hand."

After the oath, Mil and I signed property forms, shook hands, and were led to another office where the ME was waiting.

We talked to the ME, and when we walked out, the day was still bright. The prison yard was full. Desolate men stared at us from behind the mesh wire walls. One or two wolf-whistled, another begged for cigarettes. We got into the car, both of us quiet, and spent time thinking our own private thoughts on the car ride back home. Mil finally broke our silence.

"Lucky thing," Mil started, "rather, good thing you wiped the corner of our victim's mouth with that Q-tip."

"Yeah. Testing positive for cyanide certainly would indicate foul play," I said.

"You think?" Mil replied.

We both laughed. "Detective school 101," I said.

"Two to five weeks is a long time to wait on the full tox screen."

"We'll see if the sheriff has any pull. That could shorten things." I paused. "In the meantime, we work it as if we know she was murdered by poisoning and that the cause of death was cyanide. We go through all the party photos and statements. Someone gave her that cyanide at the party. We just have to find out who."

"Who and why," Mil said. "There's a motive we just haven't nailed down."

"How does one go about securing cyanide?"

"Another detail to run down," Mil replied.

"There's other perpetrators to consider," I said, "outside of the party guests."

"What?"

"After the reasoned discussion of alternative theories of the case by Deputy Sheriff Barbee, we have to check for any MS-13 crossover."

Mil laughed. "That guy, doesn't he know the only gang operating in our active adult community is the pickleball club?"

"The Mah Jong mob?" I added.

"Don't forget The Sacred Order of Pilates," she said.

"The HOA is the real criminal behind everything."

"True that," Mil said. "True that."

Troy Trips With Maryann

Maryann uncrossed her legs and took three more deep breaths of the crisp fall air before she opened her cornflower blue eyes. Her sister did not have a meditation area, but the cozy back sun porch was a welcome escape from the unsettling vibes in the main house. Maryann sighed. She supposed that ripples were to be expected. Bethann's spirit could not be at rest when the living were unsure how she died. A shudder ran up Maryann's straight spine.

Even as teenagers, Maryann knew Bethann's ruthless self-interest was going to be her undoing. Countless times, the jilted boyfriends would seek Maryann's consoling words. Once when Bethann turned, after yet another cruel phone conversation flattening her latest admirer, Maryann could see the jagged red flashes of her aura. The undercurrent of black edging concealed turbulent

186

emotions. The fiery red exuded confidence and extended more toward greed. Being her sister, it was disturbing to look so much alike and be so very different inside.

Seeking relief from unhappy memories, Maryann's generous lips slowly stretched into a half smile. She rolled her shoulders once to hear the crackle run down her back. She then stood and walked toward the entry table where she'd dropped the rental keys. The van would be a great escape today. How fun it had been to ask the rental agency clerk what vehicles were available. After the young man had tossed back his spiked bangs, he gave her a languid up and down look. Noting her Earth Mother attire and swinging crystal necklace, he said, "I've just the ride for you!" He brought out the latest VW Van retro California body style. It was a flashback to her happier days.

Of course, in those early days, vans were not electrically powered. Maryann was all for helping the environment. However, not until Maryann drove off the lot did she remember that Bethann's garage did not have a charging station. Fortunately, the van's screen identified an electric charging station in the neighborhood Club's parking lot. Today, changing energy was on the agenda, she thought on the way.

"Blast," Maryann muttered. She had forgotten to verify which side of the van had the charging plug outlet. She backed out of the space and drove around the lot again to realign the VW's outlet with the charger station.

Meanwhile, across the parking lot, the doors to the Event Center kept opening and closing as multiple residents entered and exited, signaling the beginning and end of classes.

Troy Danville walked out, shifting his gym bag higher on his broad left shoulder. Today had been a welcome workout. He had beaten the crap out of the gym's heavy bag. Solid swings landed where he pictured his son-in-law's face. While walking the four rows to where his car was parked, he noticed a VW van circling near the charging station and stood to watch the driver's efforts. Suddenly, yards of peasant skirt and loose blouse rolled out of the van. He smiled and had a feeling this was not going to be an easy connection.

Sure enough, looks like a damsel in distress in the parking lot, Troy thought. Pumped up from his rigorous early morning gym routine, he strolled over to lend a hand or anything else that might be needed. "Technology is not always our friend," he said to the woman's back. "Here, let me try," he easily took the plug out of her hand.

When Maryann turned and faced Troy, he dropped the connection onto the asphalt. Taking a half step backward, he was silhouetted against the white van panel.

Maryann narrowed her eyes and saw his aura of sensual orange tinged with defiant red leadership shift into a fuzzy yellow outline. Here was a man in need of physical and mental balance in his life, she thought. Intrigued, she tipped her head to one side and waited for what was becoming the inevitable comparison to her sister Bethann's appearance.

"Oh, you look so much like..."

"Yes, I know, my sister Bethann. I am Maryann, here sorting out the estate details. Apparently, also struggling with electrical issues." She bent to pick up the connection at the same time Troy recovered and reached for the plug. They bumped heads.

"Well, could this get any more awkward?" Troy asked as he rubbed his forehead. He plugged the charger cord into the van's outlet.

"Let's hope not!" Maryann chuckled as she pushed her hair away from her cheek.

Attempting to regain his composure, Troy asked, "Yours?" He ran a hand along the chrome trim that slid around the VW's retro body curves.

"No. On the rental lot, it called to me. Good times. Good memories."

"I bet. Remember, if the van is a rockin', don't come a knockin'!" They both laughed heartily.

"I just need to get some fresh air and inhale more deeply, if you catch my drift. Any ideas?" Maryann waited for Troy to offer suggestions.

Troy cleared his throat and then winked. "The Indian Casino has special laws, not just regarding gambling. It would be a hoot to roll up in this van and watch the expressions. It's about two plus hours away."

"Not sure I would be comfortable not knowing the back roads. Do you offer escort, I mean, travel services as well as car charging lessons?" asked Maryann.

"Absolutely! When?"

"Live in the present is my motto. It seems like the dealership had a pretty good charge on the battery already. In a few minutes, it should be full. Would you stay here while I make a quick trip to the ladies?"

"Certainly." Silently, Troy thanked his lucky stars that he had showered and dressed in street clothes after his workout. This was fortuitous and a bit dangerous. Yet, Maryann seemed to be the polar opposite of her sister Bethann. Anyway, what was the harm in having a little fun? For the first time in weeks, he felt excited and adventurous.

As Maryann settled into the driver's seat, a chill washed over Troy. Damn. He had not said anything sympathetic about Bethann's death. His stomach clenched at his oversight. "Oh, um, just realized I had a lapse of manners. Sorry, you have to deal with your sister's death."

Maryann nodded and turned to Troy. "We all must deal with the cycle of life. How we each cope makes all the difference." She noticed a shift both in Troy's aura and demeanor. A pulsating blue ripple edged around his throat chakra. She waited for him to share.

"Yeah. My wife, I, well, I was widowed not so long ago. Some days are harder than others."

"Then let's make this one of the easy days." Maryann smiled and rolled on toward their destination.

The Wrath of Naomi Kahn von Hapsburg

Naomi could not stand to be at home any longer than necessary. The blood stain on the kitchen floor was a stark reminder of the tragedy that had befallen her. As she had suspected, hiring a new maid would not be easy. The last one to interview fainted upon seeing the stain. There was no way she would clean that up. So, the search continues, and the stain persists.

Also, Gunther insisted on staying home. He spent his time either in his so-called office or in the garage staring at the trash bins. Trash bins! He has finally lost it, she thought. "What are you staring at, old man?" she had asked.

"They look different," he had replied, shaking his head. "Don't you see? The recycle bin. It's dirty. I know the service just cleaned them. Why is it dirty now?"

"Who cares? It's a bloody trash bin, for God's sake! It

was bad enough you had to set them out last night! Why would I look at them now?"

"But..." He had gone on from there, continuing to elaborate on the subject. Naomi had shaken her head and left him to his trash receptacle obsession.

She had looked at her phone for any events at the club this morning; there had to be something she could do. Anything to get out of the house. Pilates? No, sold out. Bridge. OK, well, that's it then. How hard could that be?

Which is how she ended up in the Crow's Feet at the club. People were milling about, chatting aimlessly. It was the kind of blathering about grandchildren and doctor appointments that drove her mad. Maybe this is a mistake, she thought.

"Naomi!" she heard someone call to her. It was Kitty. Yes, this was a mistake. "I didn't know you played."

"Hello Kitty. Well, it's been some time, but I'm sure it will come back to me."

Kitty reached out for Naomi's hand and said, "Naomi, I am so sorry about what happened. Poor Carol."

Naomi fought back the urge to retake possession of her hand. She was not happy about the liberty, but she knew one must keep to the social niceties. Even with people like Kitty. "Carol? Oh, yes, the help. I am sure that's all terrible for her. Somehow, we are coping.

Gunther has taken it badly, I am afraid. Men just can't handle adversity!" She took her hand back, hoping the social niceties were at an end. Alas, no, Kitty continued to speak.

"You are absolutely right there," concurred Kitty. "Rusty is the same way. Have you heard that they banned poker games at the club? No? Well, it's true and about time. There was something about not allowing liquor sales and gambling in the same facility. So, now he just mopes around, spending all his time at his friends' houses. Probably watching sports or whatever men in the wild do."

Why does she insist on talking to me? Naomi wondered. When do we play cards? "That's nice," she said.

"Well, I've insisted that we spend more time together. We're taking my widdle Xena for a nice walk later this morning. Maybe we'll stop by and say hi. I'm sure Rusty can cheer Gunther up!"

"Oh no, that won't be—"

"Wait, who's that?" Kitty interrupted, looking out the window.

"Who, where?"

"Out there, in the parking lot, by the EV things. Isn't that Bethann? But she's dead!" Kitty paled and collapsed into a chair.

"Ah, I see," said Naomi. Kitty is such a typical woman, she thought—so weak and fragile. "That's Maryann, Bethann's sister," she said in an authoritative tone. "She just arrived to settle Bethann's estate. The resemblance is uncanny, is it not? Who would have thought that there were two of them in the world?"

"That's a relief. We don't want dead people wandering around the community. She is pretty. Have you met her?"

"Yes, briefly. Who's that with her?"

Kitty regained her composure and stood up. Squinting, she said, "Of course! That's Troy, our most eligible widower." Absently, she fluffed her sparkly hair. "Bethann's sister just got here, you say? Troy certainly moves fast."

"They are having quite the tête-à-tête," observed Naomi.

"Troy has a reputation with the ladies. A real charmer, some say." Kitty frowned. "He has always struck me as a bit shifty, though. I guess that's not unusual in manager types. Some women even like that."

"Well, I like strong men. Like my Gunther, of course."

"Look, they're getting in the van," said Kitty.

"Yes, they are. Wherever could they be off to?" Naomi smiled, her heart filling with a happy contentment, anticipating the moment to come. Poor Gunther. I can't wait to tell him that Troy beat him to the punch. What a fool chasing after Maryann! Thank you, Troy! Now I have something much more fun to do than play bridge!

"I'm sorry, Kitty. I just remembered a pressing engagement at home. Something I need to tell Gunther."

"But we are just getting set up!" protested Kitty as Naomi headed out of the room. "Well, Rusty and I will stop by later!"

Gunther regarded the recycle bin. It was different. But how? It's the same color and shape–just not as clean as he remembered. So, it's dirty. What does that matter? Naomi was right for a change. He could hear his Opa reprimanding him. "Focus!" he would have said. "Trivial things do not distract a man of substance! You have now failed twice in one simple task."

"But...it was not my fault!" Gunther protested, now fully engaged in conversation with his long-dead, hated grandfather. Will the old terror never leave me alone? "The plans were perfect! Naomi should be dead by now. Can I help it that other people got in the way?"

"Plans," he sneered. "You call those plans? Poison the mouthwash, hope she drinks it. Poison the vodka, hope she drinks it. Those are fantasies, Junge. Men of substance, we take action! We don't leave things to chance!" Opa regarded Gunther with his withering, measuring gaze, finding him deficient as always. "You are truly still a cowardly little boy, not wanting to get your hands dirty. That bit last night, wearing gloves to take out the trash. That was embarrassing! I hope no one saw you."

"You told me," Gunther protested, "I should maintain my dignity always. Von Hapsburgs do not get their hands dirty!"

"But they do, you know this. They did not hesitate to use their power as emperors to put down revolts, killing hundreds, burning their homes! They acted decisively. You and I, we are descended from them!"

"Tell me, then," Gunther pleaded. "What do I need to do? How do I kill her, finally?"

Opa smiled and waved his arms at the tools neatly hanging on the walls in the garage: hammers, saws, and shovels. "You have everything you need here. Only you must use them. You can no longer leave this to chance. No more mistakes!"

Gunther recoiled in horror. It was one thing to kill anonymously, quite another to wield the hammer. To feel bone and brain crushing from the blows. That required hatred. He didn't hate Naomi, he knew that. She just had the misfortune of being in the way, of being inconvenient.

"No, Opa. I cannot do this."

"Gunther! Where are you?" he heard Naomi's voice. "I have some news for you," she called in a sing-song tone.

"I think you may change your mind soon, Junge," said Opa, before disappearing.

Gunther collapsed in a camp chair, defeated. Can I just hide in here, quietly? Maybe she will go away.

"Oh, there you are. Still talking to your trash bins?" She walked into the garage, with a sadistic smile on her face. Naomi smiling was never a good thing. "Or maybe you are just sulking? Still mourning poor Bethann?"

"What do you want, Naomi? Why are you back here?"

"I know something you don't know. I also know what you're planning." She glared at him, then. "Yes, your land grab scheme. That's crazy, you old fool, it would never work. Even if you could leave me and marry Maryann."

"What do you mean?" he protested, his eyes wide. "What scheme? I could never leave you, Naomi. You are imagining things. Maybe we should speak to the doctor again. Adjust your medication." Gunther's lips assumed his most alluring smile. "You know you are the only one for me."

"Bullshit! I've seen how you look at Maryann. You think you can 'woo her'? Is that how you would say it, in your quaint way?"

"No, I just wanted to be of help, if I could. What happened to her sister, poor Bethann..." He began to take an inventory of the tools on the wall. The various shapes and sizes. How they might be used. They were all spotless, of course. They were just for show. A man had to have tools.

He could tell Naomi was warming up to the subject. The withering comments would soon arrive. How would I explain it? Self-defense? Momentary lapse?

"Poor Bethann, my ass. But that's OK, you have Maryann now. Don't you? Here's the surprise, you old goat. I just saw her cozy up to Troy in the Event Center parking lot before getting into a VW van with him! So, you can write off that meal ticket!"

"Troy?" Gunther was incredulous. He knew Troy hated Bethann; he'd read their messages. So, why would he have anything to do with her sister? His thoughts were spiraling. Besides, Maryann's mine. He dropped his chin to his chest. Why is everything so complicated? He felt his dream fading away again. How could I possibly compete with Troy? Do I need to kill him, too? Naomi watched Gunther's devastated face, enjoying every minute. "Yes, smart, athletic Troy," she said. "And Maryann had such a beautiful smile on her face as Troy helped her into the van." Naomi sadistically smiled as Gunther squirmed. "Hah! You've been outmaneuvered!" she said.

Gunther leaned forward, his head in his hands, working through the possibilities. Yes, Troy must die, he realized. That's obvious. He sat up and looked at Naomi, the impediment that was his wife. Opa was right. I can no longer leave things to chance. For once and for all, I need to finish this part of the plan.

"And I've had it with you, dear Gunther. I'm calling up my lawyer now, and I'll use that pretty little prenup to sue your saggy ass off! Where did I leave that phone?"

Gunther rose from the chair and walked around Naomi, placing himself between her and the door. "My dear, you need to stay," said Gunther in a surprisingly firm voice. "You have been causing me great consternation, and that's just rude. You have stubbornly refused to die."

"What on earth are you going on about? Refuse to die?" He could see her lips quiver, concern and doubt clouding her eyes.

"Yes, die. First, poor Bethann—that was supposed to be you. I poisoned your mouthwash, you see. And she drank it. Then Carol, I think that was her name, she drank the vodka I had doctored."

"You can't be serious, Gunther," Naomi said with a snort, tossing her hair. "You shouldn't make light of such things."

He sighed, thinking. Now, I must improvise. Use what

is at hand, so to speak. I think it's time I learned how to use these implements. Gunther advanced on her, taking a step toward the tool rack. "I can assure you, heart of my heart, love of my life. I am serious. Deadly serious. You know what they say—third time, lucky?"

"Just imagine it, Rusty!" said Kitty.

"Imagine what, darlin?" Rusty tried to manage Xena as she kept pulling on the leash. What are we doing out here, he wondered. I have a card game to get to; the five-hundred-dollar buy-in was burning a hole in his pocket. I need to win big if I'm going to replenish the pickleball club funds before anyone notices. Or is that one of those poop bags in my pocket?

"Troy, of course! Pay attention! With Maryann."

"Wait, who is Maryann?"

Kitty waved at the people in a passing car. "Keep up, silly. Maryann is Bethann's sister."

"Wait, she has a sister?" asked Rusty, as Xena paused and sniffed at a lamppost. Apparently, it was not to her liking. Probably some big dog had marked there. They walked on.

"Were they close?" he asked. How much did the sisters talk? Did Bethann tell her about my pickleball scheme?

"How should I know? I just found out about her today. That's why we're out here. Naomi knows about her, but she left the Bridge club in a rush before I could find out more. Their house isn't far. We'll just casually drop in."

"With Xena? Naomi will not like that."

"Well, OK. You're right, you can wait outside with my widdle precious," she reached down to pat the miniature canine.

"Just stand on the street, you mean? While y'all talk? For how long?"

"Ed's just across the street. You can visit with him."

"Darlin, why did you bring me along if—" he began. Xena let out a growl, her ears perking up. "What's gotten into her?"

"Who knows? I hear some pounding and a little yelling. Probably workmen. People are always renovating their supposedly perfect homes. You know how loud that can be. Look, there's Ed's house," she pointed. "Say hello for me." She continued walking up to von Hapsburg's house, leaving Rusty with Xena.

What the hell? He walked up to Ed's house and rang the doorbell. A woman he thought might be Mildred answered. *What is she doing at Ed's?* "Hi, is Ed around?"

"Sure. Hey, Ed! You've got company," she called into

the house. "How's it going, Rusty?" She bent down to pet Xena. "I remember this little girl. You're a pretty little dog, Xena! She seems upset."

"Be right there," Ed answered from an interior room.

"Yeah," said Rusty. "There's some bang—"

"Rusty!" A woman's voice screeched from across the street. "My God, help! She's going to kill him!"

"That's Kitty!" Rusty told Mildred, his voice frenzied, "She's at the Hapsburgs!"

Mildred pushed by Rusty. "Ed, call 911!" she yelled as she ran across the street. What the hell, thought Rusty. He picked up Xena and followed well behind Mildred. She had a head start, and I'm carrying a ten-pound dog, Rusty rationalized.

"Kitty," he yelled as they got to the open front door, "where are you?"

They heard her faint answer. "In the garage! Hurry!"

He followed Mildred through the house and noticed the bloodstain on the kitchen floor. Oh, right, he realized, the maid. Mildred had stopped at the door to the garage.

"Kitty, are you alright?" he heard her ask.

"You've got to stop her!" Kitty screamed.

Rusty came up behind Mildred and saw Naomi holding a hammer. The remains of a battered camp chair were on the floor. Too bad, Rusty thought. That was a nice one. Gunther was curled up next to it, sobbing.

"Please stop, Naomi," Gunther shouted. "I didn't mean for any of this to happen. Not really. It was just all a misunderstanding..."

"Naomi," said Mildred, her voice soft, calm. "It's all right. We're here. You're safe. You don't need the hammer anymore. You can put it down."

Rusty heard sirens heading towards the neighborhood. He noticed Ed coming quietly into the house.

"He tried to kill me!" said Naomi, frowning. "Three times!"

"What do you mean?" asked Mildred, slowly advancing in hopes of putting herself between the couple.

Naomi's hands trembled, barely holding onto the hammer. "Poison! Of course, Gunther never does anything right. He killed Bethann and our maid instead! Ha! You incompetent little man! Then he came after me with this!" She shook the hammer at Gunther. "Luckily, I got it away from him. He doesn't have much of a grip—arthritis."

Gunther murdered Bethann, thought Rusty. Wow! Lucky for me, y'all will stop looking my way.

"Please, dearest," said Gunther, slowly unfurling himself and sitting up. "I wasn't thinking straight. In the end, I could never kill you. Maybe that's why I always failed. You and I, heart of my heart, we understand each other in ways no one else does. These other people, they aren't important."

Boy, he can lay it on thick, observed Rusty. But then, he's probably right. They are two of a kind. He saw Mildred moving slowly up to Naomi. Ed made his way into the garage and motioned for Kitty to go back into the house.

"Rusty," he whispered. "Mil knows what she's doing. Hang back here with me."

Gunther slowly rose and held his hands out to the side, palms out. He smiled at Naomi. "You are my one true love."

"You bastard!" cried Naomi. "You think you can win me over with sweet words? Trying to kill me was bad enough. I know you were chasing after that ditzy Maryann. As if she could be interested in a man like you! She went off with a real man–Troy."

Well, Troy is a smooth operator, thought Rusty. Good for him, he needs someone after his wife died in that freak accident.

Mildred reached out. "Naomi," she said. "You don't want to hurt him, not really. The police are on their way. We are here. You are safe. Please, give me the hammer." She lightly touched the hand holding the hammer. "Let go."

Naomi nodded and handed the hammer over. "Gunther's right, you know." She looked over at Rusty, Ed, and Mildred. "None of you understands us. We love each other in our own way." She looked back at Gunther. "Why didn't you tell me? I would have helped you. Together, we could have done anything. Now, we have nothing." Her eyes teared up.

Mildred led Naomi back into the house. Ed nodded at Rusty, and they walked over to Gunther. "Gunther," Ed said, "are you OK?"

"What, me? I'm fine. Just a minor spat, you know how it is. A lover's quarrel. You can go now. We'll be fine."

"Sure, sure, Gunther. Just come inside with us."

Gunther stopped and looked over at the trash bins. "Do they look odd to you?" he asked. "The trash bins? They look different, somehow."

"No," said Ed. "They're just trash bins."

As they led Gunther into the house, Rusty said, "Congrats, Ed! Looks like y'all got your man!"

Ed looked at Gunther and then back to Rusty, "I'm not so sure about that."

Ghosts of the Past

Mildred turned the key to her front door, entering with a sigh of relief. Gunther's arrest would tie up at least one loose end. In the bathroom, she splashed cool water on her face in hopes her old habit would help calm her. It didn't. Her hands still tremored slightly from the standoff with Naomi. The situation hadn't been particularly dangerous, she reasoned, but her nerves felt jangled nonetheless.

Standing on her low step stool that she'd dragged out from beside the washing machine, she reached far back into the high cupboard, feeling for the bottle of bourbon. Mil wasn't a regular drinker but kept a pint of Old Grandpappy's around for visitors and her occasional medicinal need. That's how she thought of it. Medicine. Though she didn't really understand some people's need to continually bend their elbows, she had nothing against

207

the habit either. She had to admit, however, that it did have a calming effect on her, and right this moment she required calming.

Mildred sat in her favorite chair in the sunroom and sipped the dark maple colored liquid. She tipped the glass, debating whether to open that internal door, summoning all the ghosts. Most days, she was content to let them go about their business, uninterrupted, but incidents like today seemed to set their chains rattling. Whenever that happened, she had to decide whether to spend her energy keeping them quiet or consciously grant them an audience. She absently ran her fingers over the scar, then stopped when she realized what she was doing. I guess they've invited themselves in, she mused.

Her memory of the accident, or incident, however one wanted to phrase it, was sketchy at best. She knew most of what she knew about it from reading her colleagues' reports. What rarely left her memory, however, was the time spent in the hospital after the surgery. Or, she should say multiple surgeries, since that's what it took. Mildred had the added complication of being sensitive to narcotics, so while the IV drip of morphine was adequate pain relief in the beginning, the staff took it away after a few days. That's when the fun began. It was about the same time she developed the habit of clenching her jaw, which of course, caused more pain in the long run.

The bourbon began working. She felt her muscles relax, her breathing reverting to deep and regular rather than shallow and erratic. After Ninth Avenue happened, she met with the counselor as required before she could return to duty. It was difficult to let down her guard and approach anything resembling vulnerability, though, so their conversations had been little more than vapid. After a while, it became a standoff. She wouldn't capitulate and weep and moan to his satisfaction, and he refused to write her the recommendation to return to her previous position. Her boss had given her the option to ride a desk, but the longer she'd thought about it, the more appealing just packing it in had seemed. At the time, she was only fifteen months away from full retirement from the force anyway.

Mil swirled the glass and looked down at the movement. She exhaled loudly. The turbulence had begun when she trusted Georgie, that little weasel of a snitch. It wasn't that she leaped on the information straight away. No, Mil had done her homework and tried to corroborate what the skin and bones grease monkey had told her. She'd called her old buddy Mike, an investigator with the ATF division, to see if he could put the information in perspective. He seemed to think she'd gotten it right, based on what some of his own sources had told him. So, she went ahead and called out the cavalry.

Time and time again, she replayed the scene in her head. Mil felt the familiar jaw clenching tighten and the inevitable buzz in her ears begin. The team thought they'd be stinging The Piranha, as he liked to be known, an up-and-coming dealer groomed on the project's playgrounds who now controlled a good-sized turf in the west end. What no one had either known, or thought to tell Mil, was that the big P had recently taken to using members of his large extended family to run interference.

Mil spent most of those days in the hospital kicking herself for letting her emotions override her training when she saw the young teen being beaten to a pulp on the warehouse floor. The perp ran back into the shadows when she called out, and knowing her team was covering her, she ran to the boy's aid. He was breathing but unresponsive. 'It's OK, you're going to be alright,' she had whispered, 'I'm with the bureau. We'll get the wagon here for you, pronto.' When he opened his eyes and grinned at her, she was so surprised, given the amount of 'blood' matting his hair and dripping into his ear, that she barely felt the blade.

Now, one kidney down and several feet of intestine lighter, most days she felt like if she trusted the face in the mirror, she was doing well. So, when Naomi (Naomi, for crying out loud) waved that hammer around, she knew better than to let down her guard. But that kind of vigilance comes with a cost. Mil took another sip and let the burning liquid trickle down her throat. She knuckled the base of her skull on either side of her neck, willing the tissue to relax.

What bothered her the most was both the knowledge that horrible things continued to happen out there, and she was no longer in a position to do much about it. It seemed odd, but these two murders had felt rewarding in a sense. Like she was donning the uniform again–so to speak–and getting back on the horse. Admitting that she associated even a little positive feeling with someone else's trauma gave her pause and brought on the ever-familiar guilt.

A Gamble and a Windfall

Troy leaned back in the VW as it rolled through the higher mountains along I-40. They had stopped in Asheville at the Moose Café for a quick bite before heading west. With only an hour to go, he had offered to drive, but Maryann reminded him that she was the only one on the rental agreement.

"It would be just my luck that something would happen with you at the wheel," she said, "leaving me to pay through the nose or even have to deal with a lawsuit."

"Wouldn't happen," Troy said. "I'd take care of any costs."

"And I'd get black-balled from further rentals," Maryann laughed, then drove in silence for the next twenty minutes while Troy enjoyed the dramatic cliffs in the valley they were driving through. After his vicious punching bag workout, this relief was almost zen-like. Breaking the silence, Maryann said, "You wouldn't have to do that."

Troy frowned at Maryann, wondering what the heck she was talking about. "Do what?" he said.

"Pay for any costs if something happened to the rental. It seems Bethann was better off than I knew."

"Really? How so?" Troy straightened in his seat, knowing he had significantly contributed to that bitch's bank account.

"A recent windfall of...Oh look!" Maryann pointed to a sign reading 'Exit Here' to the casino. "Cherokee is just a few miles down the road. We're almost there!" Maryann was practically bouncing in her seat! "I've always wanted to go to a casino in a real Indian town!"

Troy didn't hear much beyond the bank account comment. He grimaced, knowing full-well where Bethann had gotten that recent windfall. Then, his mind churning, he started to smile, thinking, Bethann's demise removed the blackmail threat to my son-in-law, and now, if I play my cards right, his smiling eyes looked Maryann up and down, I could get my money back and more.

"Look at the charming shops. We just have to stop after the casino," Troy heard Maryann say. He realized then that she had been talking the entire time he'd been thinking about Bethann's blackmail funds.

"Yes, definitely. We have to stop," he said, "and

spend all the money we're going to win." They laughed heartily as Maryann pulled into the Casino parking lot. Once inside, they picked up their Caesar's Reward Player's card and took cash out of the ATM.

"Where should we start?" Troy turned to ask Maryann who was already heading toward a bank of slot machines. "Whoa, slow down," Troy said. "I thought you said you've never gambled before?"

"You didn't listen," Maryann playfully poked him in the chest. "What I said was, I've never been to a casino in a real Indian town like Cherokee, before."

"Ah hah! I guess I'll have to pay closer attention," he said, laughing. "So, where're you headed?"

"I like the machines. The penny slots are my favorite although I sometimes play the nickel or quarter slots. I'm not inclined to take big risks when it comes to losing my money."

"A conservative gambler," Troy said. "I like that."

"How about you?" Maryann slowed near the third row of penny slot machines, waiting for his reply.

"Blackjack's my game, but I'll do the slots with you."

"Oh, don't worry about me. Go play your game. You'll do well today," Maryann said.

"Oh yeah? You psychic or something?" Troy asked.

"It's your aura. It never lies," she said.

"So I'm glowing green?"

"No, not green, unless you have something that needs healing!" she laughed. "Gold and yellow are more like it. Now go! Get outta here! I'll be sitting by the slots when you get back. I could play them all day and into the night."

Troy hesitated. He wanted to spend time with her and get to know her better. But there is the long car ride home, he rationalized. "You sure you don't mind? I do love the game."

"Go! Have fun. Win some money for dinner on the way home!" she told him, winking.

"Who needs luck when I'm glowing gold and yellow?" Troy laughed. And with a wave, he headed toward the card room and the Blackjack tables.

Four hours later, Troy came bouncing back to the slot machines with a huge smile on his face. "Well, Miss Maryann," he said, "I can see you meant it when you said you could sit at these machines all day."

"Yes, and I'm about done. How'd you do?"

"Well, you, my dear, and your aura business, must be my good luck charm. I won more hands than not, this time, and cashed out nearly six big ones!"

"Whoa! That ought to buy us a really nice dinner," Maryann said, laughing.

"Now wait a minute. You haven't told me how much

you won," said Troy. Maryann shook the almost empty bag of change.

"So sorry, Maryann. Not a good day for slots, huh?"

"Maybe," Maryann smiled mischievously. "I haven't turned in my player's ticket yet. I'm guessing you didn't beat me by much."

# # #

Maryann drove the VW out of the casino parking lot and was heading down main street when Troy saw a big CLOSED sign in the window of the Smoky Mountain Cannabis Company store. "Oh crap!" He hit his head and scowled. "The store is closed. I screwed up. I am so sorry!" He had been looking forward to seeing just how unwound and pliable Maryann might become with substance assistance.

"For what?" Maryann said.

"Only the main reason you wanted to come to Cherokee—to pick up the real deal." Troy looked over at Maryann, who didn't seem ruffled at all. "Wait! Why aren't you saying anything? Aren't you pissed at me?"

"Maybe," Maryann said with a smirk on her face. "When I came over to remind you, you were laser-focused on your Blackjack hand. I hated to bother you."

"What do you mean, you hated to bother me? Isn't shopping why we came to Cherokee?"

"Listen, Troy, I don't need you or any male to hold my hand when I want something."

"Whoa! Miss Independent!" Troy frowned at Maryann as she drove the van toward the highway. "So, what are you saying? Did you go shopping while I was playing 21?" Maryann just smiled.

"Why, you little sneak. What did you get?"

"Look under the back seat," Maryann said.

Troy gazed around the headrest and whistled at the size of the package stuffed under the back seat. "Holy shit! What did you do? Buy out the entire store?"

"Like you said, Troy, it was quality merch. Passing up that kind of opportunity would have been insane, especially after cashing in my wins. The penny slots never fail me!"

Troy reached back, picked up a package, and started to open a bag of gummies.

"Put that back," Maryann said. "You failed to mention that you can buy gummies in Cherokee, but you can't take them off Cherokee Nation land. So, that means..."

"That means what?" Troy asked.

"That means you get nothing until we get back! Besides, you owe me a dinner, 'a nice dinner on the way home,' you said."

Secret Agent Man

Billy Dan saw Maryann and Troy alternately laughing and looking puzzled in the Club's parking lot. Since Bethann's death, he had been keeping a close eye on his remaining sister now that she was in town. He wasn't altogether pleased to see her conversing with Troy. He was even less thrilled when they jumped into her electric VW bus and drove toward the exit gate.

A fat raindrop fell on his head, and he turned his palms up, critically craning his neck to the sky. It always rained in North Carolina; the question was how much?

"Watch it!" a woman's voice barked. He stopped short, gasping. "Crazy old coot," she muttered, glaring as she marched around him on the sidewalk. This is why I don't venture out much in the daytime, he thought.

BD briefly considered wandering over to Troy's house now, seeing as how he was obviously not there.

Then decided against it even though he was running low on those good Cuban cigars Troy kept 'locked away' in his humidor. Locked. Yeah, right. He snickered. No telling when Troy would return home, and he didn't want to chance it. Oh, what the hell!

With the Secret Agent Man refrain "they've given you a number and taken away your name," blasted from the Club's soundtrack fading behind him, he trudged down the winding sidewalk through the stand of trees, eager to get to the main walking path ringing the property. He hadn't anticipated an opportunity to score some more smokes this afternoon and would need his fluorescent lemon-lime vest. It was what all 'Blight Spew's' landscape crew wore as they tramped through the neighborhood running every noise-making machine known to man. They turned up unannounced, or rather, on whatever day their weekly schedule indicated they would be elsewhere, and roamed the streets, sidewalks, berms, and backyards at will.

It was of little concern to them whether there was actual work to be done, so long as they could wander around with jet engine loud gas-powered leaf blowers or drive their riding mowers up and down the streets instead of loading them on trucks for transport. BD imagined there must be actual crews who did the work, since some work did get done, along with duplicate crews that roved around pretending to work in order to run up the fee. No doubt Blight Spew's financial manager and the HOA's office worker in accounts payable were related.

Back at the treehouse, Billy Dan rummaged through the footlocker until he found the vest and stuffed it into a Harris Teeter shopping bag. He'd be able to secret the bag away in the large pocket of his cargo pants to avoid attracting attention. From his array of hats hung on nails along the wall, he selected a straw hat sporting the largest brim to blend in with the workers. One or two people might wonder at his grayish white beard, but like most of the self-absorbed, wealthy population, residents here didn't tend to pay much attention to their groundskeepers. Finally, he picked up the weed whacker from the small shed he'd built at the tree's base. The implement didn't have a string inside anymore, which is why he'd found it in someone's trash bin one night. He hadn't been exactly sure why he thought it might come in handy. Now, sure enough, he could use it.

Troy's house was still quiet. BD lingered near the driveway for a few moments, listening for any sign of activity. Finding none, he crept around to the back. The house was near one of the paths leading up from the woods and backed up to a bank of trees. It sat on a curve, so unless Troy's immediate neighbors were outside, it was unlikely anyone would see him. He puttered around the back patio's perimeter, running the weed whacker along the edge. Gradually, he worked his way closer and closer to the back door. Between the tiki bar on one side, a tea olive hedge on the other, and the back entrance recessed between two wings jutting out into the yard, he was certain he wouldn't be seen. He knocked on the glass slider, then rapped again. Nothing.

The pick worked its magic. And the door rolled open. Geezus, he thought, shivering. Way to stick it to the environment, Troy. Crank up the AC, even when you're gone. Wiping his shoes on the mat, he stepped carefully into the room. The humidor was near the Butler's Pantry. A sound from outside made him pause mid-stride, and he stumbled forward, cracking a shin on the side table. BD froze. An engine rumbled low. Was it someone pulling into the driveway? He'd thought Maryann's rented bus was an EV, so it wouldn't make the kind of vehicular low growl favored by men who needed to compensate for lack of natural endowment. Billy Dan looked around. He could dash into a bathroom if need be. Or he could just leave now and hope he made it out in time. But he really wanted another one of those exquisite cigars. A rustling noise outside near the front door caused his insides to clench. A shadow wavered through the frosted glass. Thud! Oh, a delivery.

He realized he'd been crouching low and straightened up. As he waited for his heart to stop dancing the mambo in his chest, he contemplated resting a while after all the excitement. As lean and relatively fit as he was, he was still an old man. Pausing again in Troy's living room, he thought better of it. His mouth had gone dry, though, and he couldn't seem to get the saliva flowing. If one of his coughing fits started, who knows how long he'd be here. He might still be doubled over on the rug when the garage door opened for real this time. A glass of water would do the trick.

The tap wouldn't run cold, and he distrusted those built-in water lines in most refrigerators these days. If people didn't use them enough, they could grow mold. And then there was that horrible black gunk that flowed freely out of so many faucets. BD suppressed a shudder and opened the refrigerator door. Surely, Troy won't miss a swallow or two of orange juice or whatever else was in there.

He gazed into the cold maw of the appliance, puzzled. There was a pitcher of something pink, probably cranberry juice or pink grapefruit, but it was the little vials crowding the back of the shelf that caught his attention. What were those? First things first, he thought, hauling out the pink liquid. He sniffed. Cranberry, or maybe Hawaiian punch. Did anyone over the age of six really drink that? Not wanting to dirty a glass, he tipped some of the sugared water into his mouth. Ahh, better. Careful to replace the pitcher in the exact spot he found it, he stretched his hand to the back of the shelf.

His vision wasn't what it used to be, but he thought he read 'insulin' on one of the small bottles' labels. Not anything that interested him. Many folks needed it, and he counted himself lucky not to be one of them. He glanced out of the window, noting the rain beginning to fall. Better amscray before being caught skulking around in a lemon lime vest and sun hat.

Trembling, he opened the humidor on his way back to the living room. With all the trouble he'd gone through, only one seemed hardly worth the effort. He took two.

The Morning After

Dinner at the Inn was...well, nice doesn't do it justice. The dining room was elegant, and the food was delicious beyond description! Troy had called from the van at the same time as the Blue Ridge room had a cancellation. "Our luck continues," he had said.

Following dinner, the two-hour drive from Asheville to home seemed to take forever. Thankfully, traffic was light in the late hour. Troy talked constantly on their way back, partly to keep Maryann awake, but mostly because he enjoyed talking to her. He couldn't remember a recent time when he'd enjoyed himself more.

Back in the community, Maryann pulled the VW into the parking lot near the Event Center where, hours earlier, their day had begun. "Which car is yours?" she asked, driving slowly between lanes.

"Oh, I didn't drive this morning," Troy said. "Walking

to the center is my before and after workout routine. I do it every day. You'll have to drive me to my house."

"Now there's a come-on if I ever heard one," Maryann said, laughing. "Tell me where to go."

Fifteen minutes later, Maryann found herself sitting with her right leg tucked under, on the love seat in Troy's great room, a bag of gummies open on the coffee table, and a drink in hand. Alexa was quietly playing old Sinatra love songs.

"I haven't felt this relaxed in a long time," Maryann said.

"Glad to hear that," Troy responded as he slid onto the loveseat next to her. He raised his glass, and they clinked. "This has been an absolutely lovely day."

"Agreed," said Maryann and offered her glass for another clink. "Thank you so much for the trip to Cherokee," she said, yawning. "I'll always remember it."

They sat silently, each sucking on a gummy, listening to the crooner sing one love song after another. Troy moved closer and put his arm around Maryann. Her eyes lost focus as she snuggled closer and rested her head on his shoulder. Then, just as suddenly, she jumped up and pulled on Troy's arm. "Get up, lover boy, get up. I want to dance!" Barefoot, she spun around, her skirt swirling high, revealing long, tanned legs.

Troy licked his lips and staggered up to her side. They clung together, moving back and forth to the music.

When the music stopped, they kept swaying until Maryann pressed her hands on Troy's chest, grabbed either side of his shirt collar, and said, "Troy-ish, you-ss a migh-ty fine danz-zer." Then she giggled and stumbled to the couch, pulling Troy down on top of her. "I bets you-ss a migh-ty fine ka-iss-er..."

Troy's head was spinning. Just who was in control here? He blinked at Maryann's lips, so close, trying to focus. Giving up, he pressed his mouth to hers. "Bethann," he murmured. Maryann moaned as their tongues touched.

With that, Troy lost all sense of the present. In the midst of drug induced passion, he thought Bethann was in his arms. "What are you doing here? I sshppiked your drink...you're s'posed to be dead!"

"What you say-ing, T-roy?" Maryann socked him in the shoulder. "I'm Ma-Ma-ry-ann! M-a-r-y-a-n-n! Not Bethann!"

# # #

They awoke the next morning to the sound of garbage trucks clunking down the street.

"Oh God! Oh, God," Maryann said as she pushed

Troy's bare leg off of her and sat up. Reaching for her thong, she stretched her cramped legs and said, "I can't believe we fell asleep."

"Man, that weed was really potent," said Troy, smiling. "Want to try another go-around?"

"No! No! No! I need to get back to Bethann's." Maryann pulled her shirt over her head and reached for her skirt. "I'd really like to leave before too many of your neighbors get the wrong idea."

"Wrong idea? Like what? Like we were screwing all night long, maybe?"

"Stop it!" Maryann giggled, grabbed Troy's shirt off the floor, and threw it at him. "Get dressed. I have to leave. The VW in your driveway is a give-away, besides, I need to go through some boxes before that detective comes this afternoon."

Troy heard the word, detective, and sat up. "A detective? Which one?"

"The woman, I think. She said she had a few more questions for me, not that I can tell her much. Bethann and I hadn't talked for a long time, as you know."

Maryann backed out of Troy's driveway and almost hit Steve, the good neighbor who moved everyone's garbage bins back by their garage. His long white hair lifted in the breeze as he stopped and waved.

"Great," Maryann said to herself. "So much for missing the neighbors!"

# # #

After a quick shower and light breakfast, Maryann hummed as she opened the top drawer of her sister's desk. With the wastebasket beside her, she began to sort through things, her mind reflecting on her day in Cherokee with Troy. He really is charming, she mused, and handsome. Maybe, after I get Bethann's house in order, I'll just move here instead of selling. They do seem a little too bourgeois for me, but then, everyone has been so nice. I'll have to start paying more attention.

Inside the middle drawer of Bethann's desk, Maryann found an odd-shaped key tucked into a small envelope.

"Humph? I wonder what this opens?" She looked around. The file cabinet drawers were all unlocked and open. Turning back to the antique desk, she noticed an equally odd-shaped keyhole in the bottom drawer. Pulling on it proved futile. Removing the key from the small envelope, she tried it in the lock and heard a click.

The drawer popped open, revealing several file folders marked 'Private'. The first one had a list of names, dates, and what looked like events, penciled in. Maryann thought

229

some of the names sounded familiar; names she's heard since arriving.

"Hmm?" she muttered.

The next folder included a stack of letters with copies of canceled checks stapled behind. Big checks. Maryann's eyes grew wide as she paged through them.

"What the heck, Bethann? What were you up to?"

She was about to close the folder when she noticed the name, Danville, Terrance Danville. She looked up, trying to remember why that name sounded familiar. Then she flipped the page. Stapled behind was the copy of a cashed check for fifty thousand dollars made out to Bethann, written by none other than Troy Danville!

"Shit! Shit! Shit! Now, why would Troy be writing Bethann a check for that kind of money?" Maryann jumped up and paced the room, talking to herself. "Last night. Last night, Troy called me Bethann and said something else. What was it? Come on, Maryann, think!"

Just then, the doorbell rang.

A Caterer's Clue

Maryann hurried to the front door, clutching the thick folder. She could see through the frosted glass that Mildred stood on the porch, and Ed was her shadow. Maryann flipped the door lever down hard. Swinging the door open wide, she almost shouted, "Well, come in!"

Mildred gave Ed a frowning glance and shrugged her shoulders as they followed the marching Maryann into the dining area. He used his practiced blank face to wait to hear more. Maryann slapped the folder down on the dining table. Mildred blinked twice. The folder slid on the mahogany surface and rested on the edge in front of Ed.

"You two are working for me, or so I thought."

"We are, Maryann, we are," Mil said.

"In fact, yesterday morning we were officially assigned to your case," Ed said as he slowly nudged the folder to a safer position and opened it. "What have we here?"

231

"This morning, I opened a locked drawer in my sister's desk and found that!" Maryann pointed a shaking finger at the folder.

"Names, dates, checks of various amounts from lots of people. Some are significant sums." Maryann crossed her arms and held her elbows to steady her breathing. "Did you know about this? This money-making venture of my sister's?"

Mildred quietly cleared her throat and nodded. "We knew Bethann was pushing neighbors for money based on texts we downloaded from her phone. How much and for how long, we weren't entirely sure. Did she ever say anything to you about this?"

"No! Damn it! One of the checks, for the largest amount, is from Troy. Yeah, Troy, the charmer I just spent a day and most of a hazy night with. There, now just you and the garbage gent know."

"Who?" Ed's face shifted to puzzlement.

"Oh, the long white-haired Santa Claus who hauls everyone's emptied bins from the curb up to garages." Maryann released an exasperated huff of air. "Never mind that. Why didn't you tell me about Troy? I'll have to cut that off immediately."

"Wait. Let's not be hasty." Mildred held her hands up, open-palmed. "You have an association with Troy that we can use to your advantage. He doesn't know that you're aware of the money schemes."

"Mil's right, Maryann," Ed said. "Even though Gunther is in jail, the ME informed us he did not kill your sister. No one else knows this." Eyes wide with confusion, Maryann stared from Ed to Mildred.

"You could help find out who really killed your sister." Mildred looked hopefully at Maryann.

Ed took this request as an opportunity to deflect Maryann's anger by pointing to the open folder. "All we know is that it wasn't Gunther. We're not saying it's Troy, but don't stop seeing him until we know more. Really, anyone listed in this folder has cause to end Bethann's blackmail efforts. Look, the most recent payment is from Kookie's Kitchen Katering. There is only one payment. Wonder why?"

"Yeah, we saw that in the texts," Mildred said. "Seems like we need to interview the caterer." She watched as Maryann's focus shifted from frustration to curiosity.

Mildred could smell the baking sugar from the driveway. Kookie ran her catering business out of her home. Interesting, thought the retired agent. It took several pushes on the out-of-tune doorbell before Kookie jerked the door open.

"Well, you are on time, but so are my tarts in the oven. Follow." Kookie ordered and turned toward the kitchen, painted in an overwhelming amount of bright yellow. Mildred complied.

"As you know," Mil said, "Ed Prescott and I are pulling together some facts about Bethann Cook's death. We are working for the victim's sister, Maryann, with the approval from the Sheriff." Mildred swallowed, practically tasting the air of lemon zest and graham cracker crust.

"So, what's that got to do with me?" Kookie bent to pull a rack of tarts out of one of the double ovens. The metal rack clanged on the marble countertop.

"Trivolity is full of gossips. People whose 'retired job' is to spread stories. One story was about how Bethann prevented you from winning the dessert table contract for the New Year's Eve party." Mildred waited for a denial.

Instead, Kookie said, "True dat."

"What?" Mil cocked her head.

"I applied for the New Year's contract before my North Carolina Home Bakery permit was approved. I mean, the inspector had already been in my kitchen and sampled everything I baked that day. He just hadn't filed his report. Miss high and mighty Bethann found out

234

somehow and threatened to tell the Trivolity Banquet Manager."

"So, Bethann said a little money would help grease the deal?"

Kookie smacked her lips at Mildred's clever phrasing. Indignantly, Kookie replied. "I only use real butter! Yes, money she wanted, and I really wanted that contract. Huge payday, you know. I forked over some cash once and then thought, to hell with that. The permit was bound to be issued soon. When I refused to come up with more cash, sweet Miss Bethann told the Banquet Manager about the permit situation."

"I often see your van in the neighborhood," Mildred commented.

"Sure do. I work private parties and like it a lot. Those big bashes with everyone getting drunk and rowdy aren't good for my business. No one remembers what they ate!"

"Understandable," Mildred commented. "What was it like to work with Naomi?"

"Work WITH? Are you kidding me? Mrs. Kahn von Hapsburg, as she instructed me to call her, was a Micro Manager with Capital M's. At least I had Bart to swap catering horror stories."

"Bart?"

"Yeah. Bart the Bartender. Bet his parents didn't think

of that when they named him."

"Hmmm." Mildred said. "Did you and Bart notice anything out of the ordinary about the party?"

"What, aside from that stupid Murder Mystery theme? Did that ever turn out to be a bad joke! Nah, as usual, some guests brought bottles of booze as gifts for the host and hostess. Of course, not their best. Not the pricier liquors. Man, for rich people they are cheap sometimes."

Kookie froze for an instant with her dripping spatula over the mixing bowl. Mildred knew to pause as the thought buzzed through Kookie's head and landed on her lips. "Wait a minute. I do recall one of the guys did bring a fancy bottle and made a big deal out of telling me and Bart not to touch it." Kookie returned to scraping the side of the mixing bowl.

Mildred watched the circular motion as her own thoughts swirled. She mused to herself; I wonder if that special bottle is still in the von Hapsburg's house? Or could it be resting in the swapped recycle bin in Ed's garage? "Kookie, what did the bottle look like?"

Kookie frowned and said, "I might have... It might be...in with some stuff I brought back after cleaning up. Ya want it?"

Mildred cautiously maintained a flat tone. "Sure, if you got it."

Kookie checked her oven timer, removed the thin latex gloves she had been wearing while baking, and swished out of the kitchen into the pantry. Over the sound of boxes sliding across shelves, Mildred called out. "Would you mind putting latex gloves on again? If you find the bottle, I'd like to avoid additional fingerprints.

"No problem," came her reply from the pantry. "I have another box of gloves right here on the shelf." A few minutes later Kookie returned, gin bottle in hand. "It's your lucky day," she said, handing it to Mildred. "I'm not much of a drinker. Don't even know what this stuff is. Swear I did not swill any of it!" With a low laugh, she said, "Ya know parties pay so little. Sometimes I pick up a few opened items as I clean up. Friends appreciate trying new stuff."

"I'm not much of a drinker either," said Mildred. "Oh, there's only a little missing. Would you mind putting the bottle in a bag, so your neighbors don't think we are avoiding liquor taxes?"

"Funny. Let them think what they want. I am too busy running my business to worry about their lives."

Mildred thanked Kookie for her information. She looked longingly at the tarts until one was offered. Gratefully, Mildred savored the treat as she walked to her car. Silently she concluded Kookie was as sweet, and innocent as her desserts.

Jailhouse Revelation

Gunther was becoming accustomed to the pungent odor of the backwater jail. He barely even noticed the fevered ramblings of his fellow prisoners as they spoke to fictitious people. The thought alarmed him. Imagine he, Gunther von Hapsburg, descended from the imperial families of Europe, being housed with pedophiles, petty thieves and dipsomaniacs. I'm becoming accustomed to this place because I belong here, he thought. My fall from the heights of social standing had been swift and well-deserved. Not because I committed a crime, but because I failed in the execution of my plan. This is where failures of all kinds belong.

There is comfort in belonging to this fraternity. There is comfort also in the tiny cell he now occupied. It was smaller even than Naomi's elegant bathroom, decorated in an early Spartan motif: just a bed, desk, sink and toilet.

Unlike some of his neighbors, he no longer had an imaginary presence to speak with. Opa had apparently concluded that he was a lost cause and abandoned him. Good riddance, thought Gunther.

Only one person broke his quietude—the boorish neighbor, Ed Prescott, requested a visit. At first, Gunther rejected the idea. After all, the detective is a reminder of where it had all gone wrong, the night of the party, the Murder Game. Even though Prescott lacked sophistication, he was a man of the world, and Gunther was starved for intelligent conversation. Prescott knew how the world worked. If anyone, he would understand. Gunther consented to the visit.

On the day of the visit, a guard escorted him to a small room. Prescott was already there, seated at a table. Gunther acknowledged the detective with a slight nod and sat in the chair across from him. Now, face to face, eye to eye, the prisoner noticed there was something odd about the detective's left eye. "What's wrong with your eye, Prescott?"

"Oh, you noticed," Ed replied, shifting in his chair. "A bad day, I guess. It's not usually so noticeable. Ah..." he paused. "There was an accident some time ago. It never healed quite right."

"I am sorry, Ed. Is it painful? Sometimes, a difference

can be painful. Does it help you understand better, see people differently?"

"A little, a little painful, and, yes, maybe I have a different perspective than I had before the accident. But it's not like I see auras or anything like that." He laughed, then raised an eyebrow. "You called me Ed just now, not Prescott."

Gunther shrugged, "Why not? We are the same now, you and me. I am a criminal, and you are a what? Policeman? Private detective? Yes, that's correct, a private detective. You see? Criminal, detective–two sides of a coin. There is no difference now, is there?"

"OK, I guess. Gunther, there are things I still don't understand. Even with my decades on the job. I always ask this question. Why?"

"Why what, Ed?"

That eye keeps drawing me in, thought Gunther. Seductive. Not like Bethann, of course. But seductive in the way of inviting me to talk, to confide. Maybe after Opa and Naomi, here is someone who might finally understand what I had to do.

"Why all the murders? What did you hope to gain?"

"The land, of course. It belonged to my family." Gunther's face flushed light red. "The fools lost it to the Cooks. They lost it, and then they expected me to get it back! At least the mineral rights. Is that fair?"

"Mildred and I looked into it," he said, "at the county clerk's. Bethann Cook was to inherit the rights. But why kill her? To get revenge on the Cook family?"

Gunther's hands clenched. "No, don't be absurd! Revenge is so petty. The poison wasn't meant for her."

Ed's eyes widened, then narrowed. With a vacant expression on his face, he waited for Gunther to continue. Gunther obliged. "That silly woman drank the poison instead."

"Instead?"

"Instead of Naomi!" Gunther said, his voice rising to a shout. He leaned back in the chair, unclenched his hands. He shrugged. "Ed, why do people never do what you want them to do?"

Ed shrugged in reply. "Beats me. Gina asks me the same question whenever I don't put the toilet seat down." He paused. "You said poison?"

"Yes, cyanide. Troy said it was quite effective and undetectable."

"Wait," Ed shifted forward in his chair. "Troy told you what poison to use?"

"Relax, Ed. Hypothetically only. I knew he had a military background, so maybe he would have an idea. It was a casual conversation at the Forge."

"A casual conversation? About how to kill someone?"

"Of course, happens all the time. I'm sure that even now, some group of misfits is in the Muscadine Wine Room, talking about this very thing. Troy has no idea about this. He is quite innocent."

Ed sat back. "There's just one more thing, Gunther. Your maid, Carol, died from cyanide. The vodka bottle we found in your recycle bin contained traces of cyanide. So we can link you to that death. But Bethann did not die from cyanide poisoning."

"My recycle bin?" Gunther said. "That was you! You switched them! I knew it. I'm not crazy, after all!"

"Let's not be too hasty there, Gunther. But the point is you did not kill Bethann."

"Wait, did you say I didn't kill Bethann?" Gunther slouched back in his chair, in shock. So, I haven't killed anyone, after all. No one of significance anyway. What's a maid, more or less?

"Gunther, pay attention to me now." Ed pointed his finger at his left eye, directing the prisoner's attention to it. But Gunther realized that it no longer had an effect on him; it had lost its power. Ed continued. "Who else would want to kill Bethann? She was your meal ticket? Right? Then someone ruined it for you. They cashed her in before you could. Who would do it?"

243

Gunther shook his head. "I don't know. Isn't that your job, Prescott?"

Someone else had killed Bethann, thought Gunther. All this time, I had thought that I had killed her with the poison intended for Naomi. But Prescott said no. Gunther's mind began to spin wildly. Maybe I can still get away with this, he fantasized. Perhaps Maryann is one of those women who are attracted to men in jail? This can only further enhance my allure. Perhaps I can convince Maryann to come back to me?

"Ja, Junge," said a familiar presence. It's Opa! He has returned to me! Opa was sitting to the right of the detective, where his left eye could not see. "You can still do this," Opa said, "You just need a plan."

A Gentleman Never Tells

Very little stood between Rusty and a sound sleep, but he heard Kitty get up a few times in the night. He had asked her what was wrong. All Kitty said was that she thought she had heard something like voices, and she wanted to make sure the doors were locked. He had teased her that it was probably just the guy that lived in the tree house. She was not amused.

Finally, when the sun came up, Kitty got out of bed one more time and dressed. "I'm going to take Xena for a walk. Can you brew some coffee?"

"Sure darlin, I'll get right on it," Rusty said, sitting up and scratching. "A full pot will be ready by the time y'all get back." Rusty found a pair of docker shorts and a Tripalooza t-shirt. It was fall and on the chilly side, but Rusty was a happy resident of denial. He padded his way to the kitchen, ordered up his Kingston Trio playlist on the home audio, and went about cleaning and setting up the coffee maker.

While waiting for Kitty to return and Charlie to get off the MTA, he brought up the local Trivolity Facebook page on his phone. There was nothing about last night's incident, but the moderators were strict when it came to disparaging neighborhood gossip.

"Oh well," he said, out loud, "all the better. Since I was there in person, I'll command the room at tonight's poker game." Mentally rehearsing his spotlight performance, he resumed the conversation with himself. "Sure, I seen the whole thing," he would say. "Me, afraid? Hell no, but poor high and mighty Gunther, hiding behind the chair. Good old Naomi took him down a peg or two. It was kind of funny, really, in a sad sort of way." Yep, I'll really have the jump on the news.

The front door's security chime brought him back to reality. Kitty walked in with Xena in tow. "Welcome back!" Rusty said as he started the coffeemaker. "Did you have a nice walk, darlin?"

"Pleasant enough, I guess." Kitty sat down in the middle of the oversized sectional sofa, as if she were unsure which side to sit on. Xena jumped up and snuggled up to her and happily accepted Kitty's absent-minded petting. "Rusty, can you stop the music, please?"

"Sure thing." Rusty ordered the assistant to kill the playlist. "I'm sorry you had a bad night, hon. That was dumb of me to bring up the treehouse guy. You know that's just a Trivolity legend, right?"

He poured out a cup for each of them. Kitty hadn't responded, so Rusty continued in his best concerned husband voice, "Still thinking 'bout what happened?" He added a shot of amaretto to her coffee and handed it to her. "Here, this outta help."

"Thanks, God, I hope so. I just can't help thinking about poor Naomi. I would never have thought that Gunther could do such things. He's a killer!" She took a sip of the coffee and shook her head. "You think you know your neighbors, that everyone here is decent. I guess you never know about some people."

"Hey, in a neighborhood this big, there's bound to be a few rotten apples." Rusty added bourbon to his coffee and sat next to Kitty. He put his hand on her knee.

She smiled, put her hand on his. "We're good, Rusty? Aren't we? We have no secrets from each other, right?"

"Absolutely! Darlin, you know me, I'm an open book. What you see is what you get! On the bright side, at least this is over now."

"Over?" asked Kitty.

"You know, over. They've got the killer. Ed can stop

pestering us. I mean, I like Ed–too bad I never got him to play pickleball–but he was getting on my nerves! I know Troy was really pissed at billiards night. He told me it was because that lady cop was getting up in his business. Now maybe things can get back to the way they were. Before all this."

"That reminds me. They're back," she said, sipping her coffee. "Is there any coffee cake left? I'd like something to eat with my meds."

"Let me check." Rusty got up and went to the kitchen. He searched the refrigerator, rearranging the leftovers. "Ah, yes. Here it is. I'll give it a quick nuke. What do you mean back? Who's back?"

"You know, Troy and Maryann. I told you I saw them drive off together." She sighed, "Oh, maybe I didn't. In all the...the confusion yesterday, I guess I forgot. Can you grab my pills, too, sweetie?"

"Of course," Rusty returned with the cake and their morning pills. He swallowed his with coffee. "More coffee, hon?"

"Please, and a little more amaretto this time, sweetie. They drove off together in Maryann's car–that cute yellow VW bus. You remember the kind, Rusty."

"Damn straight," he grinned. "We had some good times in the red one we had. Before we got hitched."

"Well, it's back in her driveway. I saw it there when I was walking Xena. I wonder where they went?"

"Who knows? I'll stop by Troy's and see what I can find out. Not that I'm nosy or anything–not like you busybody women." He grinned at her. "It's their business, I guess." Rusty paused and took another drink of his coffee. "Hey, he might not know what happened last night. If they were gone. I should fill him in. I'm sure he'll be glad to hear this is all over now."

"That sounds good, dear. I hope you have a nice visit." Kitty yawned. "God, am I tired. If you don't mind, I think I need to lie down for a bit." She got up, "Come on, Xena, it's nap time." She headed to the bedroom. "Say hi to Troy for me."

"Will do," said Rusty. Maybe the Ambien I slipped in with her heart meds will help her get some rest, he thought. He finished his coffee and headed out the front door. Climbing into his golf cart, he wondered how long it would take Kitty to snap out of it. Once again, he was grateful that nothing much fazed him. Kitty said it was a lack of imagination on his part. Who knows, she might be right. Is that a bad thing?

He selected the Eagles playlist on his music system and cranked up the volume for 'Hotel California'. Never too early for Don Henley. This could be the theme song for the community. 'You can check out any time you like, but you can never leave'. We've all checked out one way or the other, and we're not going anywhere. Who would want to? He sped out of his driveway. A couple of walkers on the street flipped him off as he cruised by them. 'Everyone's a critic', he thought.

Rusty saw the VW minibus parked at Bethann's, or was it Maryann's now? Will she move in? he wondered. He hoped so, for Troy's sake. If they hit it off. Troy had been so moody after Julie died. Can't blame him, of course. It was difficult to be his friend when Troy's hard, steely mood struck. He'd learned to give the widower a wide berth.

Rusty pulled into Troy's driveway. I hope they had a good time together, wherever they went, he thought. Smiling, he rang the doorbell.

After a minute, just as Rusty was going to leave, Troy opened the door. His usually well-groomed hair was a mess, and his eyes were bloodshot. He was barefoot, wearing khaki shorts and a sleeveless shirt.

"Man, you look terrible!" Rusty smiled and added, "Good time with Maryann?"

Troy stepped aside to let Rusty in. "A gentleman never tells. Besides, I don't remember much–kind of a blur. If you ever have a chance to try 'gummies', stay away from the green ones. They're not ripe, yet. Let's head out back. It's a nice day. Some vitamin D may help. What brings you here to my humble abode? I'm pretty sure that I paid my pickleball club dues."

"Hah, yeah, right. You're all paid up," said Rusty as he took a seat at Troy's Tiki bar. Troy's taste was otherwise high-end; this was the kitschy exception. Apparently, they are all the rage up north. You can take the boy out of Michigan, but you can't take Michigan out of the boy. Anyway, Rusty liked it. He and Troy spent many a fine night here. Enough that Kitty had teased him about being on the down-low with Troy, whatever that meant. So what? He enjoyed Troy's company. It was good being his best friend.

"What's up then, buddy?"

"Kitty said she saw you drive off with Maryann." Rusty raised his eyebrows, waiting.

"So?" Troy smiled, "Jealous?"

"Of course not! It's just you probably don't know what happened."

"Well, like I said, I remember some of it. Boy, that Maryann looks so much like her sister." Troy paused and frowned. "I think I may have called her Bethann."

"No shit! That's never good. When you were, you know, 'doing it'? That's bad, man. Kitty made me sleep in

251

the guest room the last time I did that."

"I...I don't know...last time? Is this a frequent occurrence for you?"

"No, y'all know I'm just funnin. Besides, once she cried out 'Xena'! Did I make her sleep in the other room? No. Anyway, that's not what I wanted to tell you. They arrested Gunther."

"Gunther? Von Hapsburg. F - me, why?"

"Murder. He confessed to killing Bethann and the maid."

"The maid? What maid?"

"The von Hapsburg's maid. Keep up, Troy. Where have you been? Oh, yeah. That's right. Anyway, Kitty and I were walking Xena, and she started barking like crazy, Xena that is, at some commotion at the von Hapsburgs. Kitty went to check it out while I got Ed and Mildred. Then, we saw Kitty and Naomi with a hammer, well Naomi had the hammer, not Kitty, and there was Gunther hiding behind the wreck of a Captain's chair, a really nice one, you know the kind that rocks and has a sunshade, you see them a lot at the club concerts in the summer. Mildred took the hammer from Naomi, and Gunther confessed and the cops took him away." Rusty took a breath.

"Oh my God! Really?" Troy lowered his shoulders a bit and ran a hand over his beard stubble. Will wonders never cease, he mused. Clearance up ahead!

"Yeah, case solved."

Troy smiled. "You know what this means?"

"No more Ed and Mildred snooping around?"

"Right, and it's boiler maker time! I've got bourbon here somewhere," said Troy, looking behind the Tiki bar. "Somehow, it's never where I left it. Ah, yes, here it is, good old Pappy. Rusty, can you grab a couple of cold ones from the fridge? It's time to celebrate! It's after noon, somewhere!"

"Roger that, good buddy!"

Rusty walked back into Troy's house and went to the fridge. Looking around, he didn't see any beer. He moved some things to the side, still no beer. Just the usual stuff and Julie's insulin vials. He wondered why his friend was holding on to the medication. It's been a year now. Oh yeah, the beer wouldn't be in the kitchen fridge. Troy had just bought a beverage fridge for the Butler's Pantry. He grabbed two bottles and went back to join Troy. "Here we go, man."

Troy opened the bottles and handed a shot to Rusty. Troy's expression relaxed. It seemed he no longer had any cares. It's good that he's hooked up with Maryann, thought Rusty. Troy's a good guy, kind of a know-it-all, and a bit prickly, at times. But I like him, and it's good to have him for a friend.

"To Bethann," said Troy, raising his glass. "Here's hoping that your sister is not the conniving bitch you were."

After two hours of his 'best friend', the boilermakers were no longer having the desired numbing effect. Troy was glad when Rusty announced it was time for him to go home and "nap" before tonight's poker game. He guided his guest back to the golf cart and sent him on his way. Rusty turned the wrong way out of the driveway. Well, buddy, maybe you should put Super Tramp on the golf cart audio system and take the long way home.

Troy went back into the house and searched the Butler's Pantry for something to at least keep the buzz going. After all, this was good news. Finally, after Julie's passing, something was going right. More than right, in fact. This calls for the Glen Moray, fifteen-year-old. He poured a shot and took a seat in the library. The Bethann problem was now more than adequately taken care of. This is cause for celebration!

"Here's to you, Gunther!" Troy raised his glass high. In a triumphant voice Troy announced "You were the perfect patsy. A few drinks at the Forge and some guidance on poisons was all it took."

He took the bait. It's so easy to get other people to do what you want, Troy thought. He took a cigar out of his collection, a Cuban, snipped the end, and lit it. Sorry about the odor, Julie. She never could stand them. He took a long drag on it. Odd, there were ten cigars last time, weren't there? There are only eight. Am I misremembering? Rusty. He must have swiped one. Or, he chuckled, it was the tree house guy.

Doesn't matter. He sipped the scotch. Yes, poor Gunther. He just can't do anything right. The murder spree sent the cops right to him. So, Bethann dead, Gunther in jail–all my problems solved. And, bonus, a chance encounter with Maryann. Troy stretched out his legs and pronounced, "Ah, yes, the world is a good place for people like me."

Maryann's quite attractive, he mused. A little ditzy, auras and all, but that's good. She'll be easy to manage. And she is really good in bed. Those gummies, though. I need to stay clear of them. It'll be tricky, he realized, a little dangerous even. I almost let it slip. Dating the sister of the woman you had just murdered. I almost gave it away.

"Risk and reward," he murmured. You can't have one

without the other. "Thank you, Gunther, for taking the heat off of me!" Troy shouted as he danced around the room and then flopped onto the love seat. I just need to be careful, he thought. At worst, there's still plenty of insulin left in the fridge. It would be a shame to have to use it, but it's good to have options.

Family Night

Troy assembled the ingredients for the marinade. The preparations for fajitas brought back so many pleasant memories. And now, finally, he could breathe again. He could enjoy life again. Rusty's news about Gunther and his confession was great. Troy looked forward to dinner with his daughter.

Steak fajitas had always been a favorite of Margot's. They had been a staple of family night when the children were still at home; she had loved trying all the different toppings and sauces. Even after she went off to Kalamazoo College, she would make the trip back at least once a month for family night.

After Margot met Daniel, she didn't come home as much. Troy had missed her, and it often brought on a melancholy mood until Julie snapped him out of it. She would tell him that when their youngest son headed off to college soon, 'it meant more time for us'.

Troy made the slits in the ribeye, poured the marinade over, and placed the marinade tray in the fridge. He rearranged the items on the shelf, placing the insulin vials further back. Then he walked into the library, settled into his favorite leather chair, and poured a short scotch.

As he continued to reminisce, he thought back to when the inevitable had happened. After graduation, Daniel proposed to Margot, and Julie went into wedding planning mode. As plant manager, Troy could easily afford the expense of the destination wedding to Maui. Nothing was too good for his baby girl. It grated on him that Daniel certainly wasn't good enough in his estimation. His future son-in-law was too full of himself, and Troy didn't trust him. Again, Julie convinced him to keep his thoughts to himself. He did. They were rewarded with two grandchildren, much to Julie's delight.

When Daniel was transferred to Charlotte, he and Julie followed. Daniel and Margot moved into an all-ages community, and they bought a house in the neighboring Active Adult community. The clubhouse was shared between the two communities, so they could see a lot of them. It was well past time for him to retire, anyway. Again, Julie said this means more time for us.

And there was more time, for a while. A picture of

Julie came up on the digital assistant's wallpaper. Troy gave the photo a respectful salute. Really, it showed both of them. They were sitting at an outdoor Tripalooza concert in the spring, just before, before....

He took a large sip of the scotch. It burned going down, bringing on a coughing fit and tears to his eyes.

"I'm sorry," he said to the picture after the coughing had stopped. The tears remained. "But I kept my promise. Margot, Daniel, and the kids will be OK now. No one will ever know what Daniel did." Troy wiped away tears. "Daniel doesn't deserve it! God help me, if he does this again...I always said he was trouble—from the first time I saw him. I was right about that. No more chances for him!" The sound of the front door's security chime shook him out of reverie.

"Hey, Dad! Where are you?" Margot called.

"Hi there! I'm in the office. I'll be right out."

"Were you just talking to someone?" she asked as he met her in the great room. She was wearing slacks and a light sweater, and a wide-brimmed hat. Margot was careful about sun exposure. Even in the fall, the North Carolina sun can be brutal.

"What? No. Probably just talking to the assistant." He smiled, happy to see her. "It never listens to me and only wants me to order stuff."

"I know, right?" she said. "I'm so looking forward to 'Family Night.'" She had brought a six-pack of some NC craft beer with her and set it on the kitchen island. "Pilsner, the guy at Total Wine said it's perfect for Fajitas."

"Sure," said Troy. He opened two bottles and offered her one. "Let's go sit outside. It's such a nice day. It should be a good day for Daniel and the kids at the ball game. I'm glad we can spend some time together!"

Margot took a seat under the large, cantilevered umbrella. After taking a drink of the beer, she narrowed her eyes and grinned at him. "So, I hear you've been stepping out. Some lady finally got her hooks into you?"

Troy flushed. "I'd hoped to tell you in person. But I guess the club rumor mill beat me to it."

"Yeah, I heard about it at Mahjong last night. The women were all upset that Trivolity's most eligible bachelor is off the market. You men have it so easy! There aren't many like you around here, fit and healthy. The women here usually outlive the men. Shit! Sorry, Dad, I didn't mean to say that."

"It's all right, kiddo," Troy said, gently. "We can't spend our lives in fear of saying the wrong thing. And you're right. I've found someone, maybe. She's very different from me. Kind of hippie-dippy, but in a fun way. I think we could be good together. We'll give it some time.

Maybe we can all get together for dinner soon."

"I'd like that."

They spent the rest of the afternoon chatting. He heard more about Daniel's job than he'd wanted to know. At least he was good at it and was up for another promotion. The girls adored him, anyway. Daughters always love their fathers, and fathers always protect their daughters. That is the way of things, or should be.

'Family Night' came to an end, and Margot said good night. Again, she said how glad she was that he had found someone. There was a parting admonition that he should slow down his drinking. She knew him well enough to know how easily he could hide being drunk. Margot didn't mention the other thing, why he should be more careful. They both knew why. It had been a good thing Maryann had declined his offer to drive the VW Bus to Cherokee.

As he returned to his library, the device shuffled the pictures again. This time, it was Julie sitting in the cherry red Porsche he had bought her for their 40th anniversary. Why not? She had deserved it. She loved it! Julie was a true driver, fearless, laughing as she left the NASCAR wannabes in the dust.

She wanted to take it on a road trip. The wineries in Yadkin Valley would be perfect. As Julie sped up Interstate 77, Troy sat quietly, hands gripping the sides of his seat. She kept to the speed limit, mostly. They stopped for several wine tastings. It was a beautiful trip.

After all that I've done, I deserve this reminder. Troy sucked air through his front teeth. "Might as well get this replay over with, again."

On the way back, they stopped for a bite to eat at the Red Herring on Lake Norman. To celebrate, Julie ordered a Smoked Old Fashioned–her favorite. They engaged in cheerful talk about the kids and the grands, about how the problem son, Sam, had finally settled down. They had floated the money for his brew pub in Grand Marais. Everyone settled. Julie was right. Now there was time for us.

On the way back to the car, Julie fumbled for the keys. "This was wonderful, Troy," she had said. "Wow, did I slur that? I think I've had way too much. You're much better at holding your liquor." She handed him the keys and kissed him. "You should drive."

I don't remember much after that, he thought. The cops said it wasn't his fault, but it always felt like his fault. The other car veered into his lane, head-on. Julie crashed her head into the dashboard. She was barely conscious as they waited for help. He told her it would be OK. As always, she knew better. "Promise me," she said. "Take care of the kids, no matter what."

"I've done that, sweetheart," he told the picture. "They're safe now."

Since then, Troy never drove if he could help it. It may not have been my fault, he thought. But if I hadn't been drinking, my reflexes might have been faster. I might have saved you. There might have been time.

Reexamining the Evidence

In the parking lot of the Scotts County Sheriff's office, Ed returned to his car and took a moment to clear things in his mind. He was not given to panic. Gunther's innocence for Bethann's death, the precipitating event in this investigation, was just a new fact to be dealt with.

Ed took in a deep breath. He thought through the jail conversation again. Having dealt with lowlifes, miscreants, and criminals his whole adult life, he had a highly developed sense of who was and was not being truthful. Part of being a good detective is developing that second sense and using it to break down the lies. Given Gunther's unstable mental condition, one would consider him an unreliable witness, but Ed did not detect any lies, only truth. Just because you're paranoid doesn't mean someone is not out to get you.

Going forward, Ed knew they had to reexamine the

initial crime scene and witness statements and come up with a renewed list of suspects. Mil was busy; otherwise, she would have been with him for this prison visit. He would give her a call to fill her in.

The Sheriff would also have to be notified that only one murder was committed by Gunther; the first was still unsolved. That was a conversation he did not welcome. Lost in thoughts of how to proceed, the trip home was a blur.

Gina met him at the entry door from the garage into the kitchen. "The return of my conquering hero," she said with a hug and kiss.

"Well," Ed said, "your greeting, though wonderful, is slightly premature. Gunther didn't kill her."

"Wait, who didn't kill who?"

"He confessed to trying to kill his wife..."

"His wife?" She shook her head. "Trying to kill Naomi?"

"Twice."

"How, who..."

"Gunther poisoned Naomi's mouthwash. He poisoned her bottle of vodka. The vodka killed Carol, the cleaning woman. She must have fixed herself a stiff one."

"I can imagine. To deal with working for Naomi and Gunther, alcohol would be very helpful." Gina paused.

"But the mouthwash and Bethann?"

"Not the cause of death." Ed reached out and touched her arm. "I mean, yes, she was poisoned, but not by the cyanide-laced mouthwash. Though some of the mouthwash was found in the corner of her mouth, it was not digested. Bethann was poisoned with the wrong type of insulin."

"Huh, what are the odds? So, Gunther tries to kill Naomi twice, doesn't kill her or Bethann, but ends up killing some poor woman trying to clean up his messy home."

Ed smiled. "Three times. He tried to kill his wife three times, if you count with a hammer in the garage."

"This is like an off-brand board game of Clue," Gina said and shook her head. "Three times. That's a lot of hate. And a lot of incompetence."

"True, but not just hate. It was premeditated, part of a plan. He wanted to get Naomi out of the way. He tried to kill Naomi the first time at the murder mystery night, all to marry Bethann."

"Bethann, for the mineral rights, right?"

"Yes. With Bethann dead, he still wanted Naomi out of the way. The second time with the poisoned vodka was for the same reason: to gain the rights now passed on to Maryann. He planned on marrying Maryann."

"Didn't Gunther realize Maryann disliked him?" Gina took a breath. "You said she physically recoiled every time he tried to touch her."

"Social and self-awareness are not attributes Gunther seems to possess."

"And the third time? With the hammer?"

Ed said, "The third time, I think he just snapped."

In his office, Ed placed a call to Mil outlining Gunther's confession and the need to find Bethann's killer.

"I have some news too," Mil said. "I'll join you as soon as I can."

The files on Ed's desk contained the statements taken the night of the murder and follow-up interviews. A collection of social media postings and photo shots, all those selfies and group pics were also on the desk. The list of suspects he and Mil had developed was short. He struck Gunther from that list and placed Naomi to the side. Ed stepped back to look at the murder board. That left just Kookie, Rusty, Kitty and Troy.

Ed began tracking their movements as reported in the interviews of the party guests. Kookie was easy; almost every reference placed her working, either behind the service table or in the kitchen. Her timeline and photos off social media matched the statements. She seemed an unlikely candidate.

Ed continued to sort and read; sure the solution was there somewhere. Seen it, felt it, heard it. He caught himself floating, his mind shifting to this and to that. Back in the day, a cup of bad, bullpen coffee, on the heat plate for hours, as thick and vicious as the acid dripping from the body of that, what...Predator? Naw. The one with Sigourney Weaver. Aliens, that's it. A cup of that coffee, unfit for human consumption and a cigarette. A Marlboro. Filtered or unfiltered. Did they come in unfiltered? Over twenty years since he quit smoking, and he still found himself dreaming, coffee in one hand and a smoke in the other. Today, he'd have to make do with a cup of watery K-pod and a stick of Trident. And then it comes to him. Rusty. He starts sorting through pictures.

Mil hurried into the office anxious to hear what Ed had found out. But before she could speak, he said, "Look at this photo," thrusting it toward her. It was a picture of Bethann, posing on the stairs, holding up a glass filled with what appeared to be a martini in mock salute. "That's a few minutes before she texted me." Mil looked at the photo and nodded.

"Now this one." Ed slid a photo over. "See in the

background, someone coming down the stairs, with the same style glass in his hand as the one Bethann brought up. It's Rusty."

"You're right, Ed. It looks the same as the one Bethann carried up." Mil picked up the other photos. "This one has Rusty going up the stairway, without a glass in his hand. Hmm."

Ed took another look at the photo through the magnifier and said, "You're right." And paused. "So, you run up the stairs, there's a woman prone on the floor, injured, dead, or dying, and your first thought is the caterer will need this glass? There is no way the caterer is gonna know it's up there. Let's make it easier for her and save the trouble of a missing glass."

"Pretty considerate of Rusty," Mil said.

"A little out of character, I'd say."

Mil grabbed a folder and pulled out a page. "Here's the blackmail figures. Note the entries next to his name. Regular payments."

"For what?"

"If I had to guess," Mil said, "infidelity. Or maybe something to do with the pickleball club. When you ask anyone about Rusty, those two things come up. Rusty? The guy tries to run the pickleball club as if he were king. And, he thinks he's a ladies' man."

The Cake is a Lie

Maryann pulled the Boston Cream Pie she had made out of the refrigerator. Beautiful, if I say so myself! I just hope it tastes as good as it looks. Carefully, she slid the dessert onto the cake holder and snapped the lid into place. She smiled, remembering how her favorite dessert usually sparked discussion about whether it was a cake or a pie. Anticipating Troy's reaction when he realizes she made the dessert herself sent a warm, fuzzy feeling snaking through her body. The passion suppressed all thoughts of Troy's contribution to Bethann's blackmail scheme. Perhaps this will take our relationship to the next level, she thought, pirouetting down the hall to get her wrap out of the closet.

Outside, a fierce wind came up, plastering raindrops to the front windows. Exiting the side door into the garage, Maryann placed the cake holder on the floor of the VW and ran back in to get an umbrella. She drove the few blocks to Troy's place, slowly dodging trash bins that spun into the road from the curb, as the wind rocked the VW from side to side. Finally, safe in the driveway, she dialed Troy's number. "You're going to have to come out and help me with the dessert. This wind is ferocious!"

"Be right there," Troy replied. Clad in a yellow raincoat that made Maryann laugh, he opened the side door and grabbed the cake holder. She opened the umbrella, and together they scurried into the house.

"Whew!" Maryann said as she shook out the umbrella and folded it up. "That was some ride over. I almost turned back home."

"Well, I'm glad you didn't. Come in. Sit down. I've chilled your favorite Chardonnay, fixed a tray of cheese and crackers, and even found a collection of Sonny & Cher tunes you might enjoy. I thought we'd relax a little before dinner," Troy said, his deep voice fluttering Maryann's insides. She smiled.

"Well now, it seems you thought of everything," Maryann said, chuckling. "But speaking of chilling the wine, the dessert I brought needs to go into the refrigerator." Maryann started to get up.

"I got it," Troy said. "I'll have to move some things aside to fit it in. You just relax."

271

"That was smooth," Maryann said. She chortled in her little girl sort of way.

"How so?" Troy yelled from the kitchen. Maryann could hear the clink of items being moved around.

"You said, 'I got it,' just as Sonny or maybe it was Cher or both sang, 'I got you babe!'"

Returning, Troy slid onto the couch next to her and said, "I do, got you, babe!" Troy silently congratulated himself on his dating prowess. Still got it, man!

The evening unfurled as Maryann had hoped. Conversation flowed easily, interesting and entertaining. Hardly one subject ended before another began. They laughed about their road trip to Cherokee; the money won, and the cannabis purchased. Troy brought out the gummies he had leftover and started to unwrap the package.

Maryann reached over to stop him. "Let's wait until after dessert," she said. "We don't need artificial means to have fun."

"You got that right." Troy leaned over and gave her a kiss on the cheek.

Maryann held him off. "Speaking of dessert, I'd say it's about time. What do you think?"

"Sounds good to me." Troy jumped up and pressed her back down onto the sofa. "You stay right there. I'll get it."

Maryann smiled to herself, what a thoughtful guy. She could hear the cupboard door open and the clang of plates on the counter as she got up and headed for the refrigerator thinking, I can serve my own dessert! In two strides, he was by her side, reaching to take the cake holder out of her hand. She staggered and almost dropped it.

"Whoa! Slow down Troy. You almost had Boston Cream Pie all over your floor!" Maryann said, chuckling.

Troy wasn't smiling. "I said, I'd get the dessert!" Troy snapped, his voice no longer friendly. He turned to close the door with his free hand. Maryann looked at him warily, the atmosphere in the room suddenly as chilly as the door he slammed shut. "I didn't know you were diabetic," she said.

"I—I, ah," Troy fumbled for words. Damn! She did see the vials.

"Goodness," Maryann said, trying to lighten the mood. "It's nothing to be ashamed of."

"I—ah. I mean, they're not mine. My wife was a diabetic. I just couldn't bring myself to pitch them," he said, trying to look embarrassed.

Maryann cocked her head, considering Troy's comment. She knew Troy's wife had been gone for more than six months. Keeping her medicine around that long seemed like a strange thing to do. Without warning, the conversation with Mil about Troy's cash contributions to Bethann's blackmail scheme crept into her thoughts. Just as suddenly, a sick feeling roared through Maryann's gut. Gasping for breath, one hand clutched her stomach as she turned and leaned against the counter.

"Are you okay?" Troy's brow wrinkled with concern.

"Yes. I think so. I just got a flash of nausea."

"May I get you some water? How about a soda? Something to settle your stomach?"

Shaking her head, Maryann said, "Thanks, but no. I'll be fine. Just give me a minute." Clutching the counter's edge, she took several more deep breaths. Troy's aura was swirling orange, yellow and green, signaling empathy and his caring concern. Maybe I really am sick, she thought.

"Okay then, if you're sure." Troy's voice was full of concern as he moved the Boston Cream Pie closer to the table.

Nodding, Maryann watched Troy take a cake knife out of the drawer and turn in her direction. "Would you like the honor of cutting the dessert?"

Maryann looked from the knife in Troy's hand to his eyes and swayed, then stepped back, breathing rapidly. "It's getting worse," she said. "I think I'd better go."

Thunder boomed as she got into the VW and rested her head on the steering wheel. All she wanted to do was to get away from this house and Troy. When she looked up, Troy was standing in the doorway, fumbling with an umbrella and looking as if he was going to come after her.

The engine sprang to life. She backed out of the driveway and headed the few blocks to Bethann's. When the garage door closed, Maryann lingered in the van trying to keep her mind from whirling. Was it just her imagination, or were things getting strange with Troy? First, there were the comments about Bethann, and then, finding his long-dead wife's insulin in the refrigerator. I mean, who does that? It's probably just a weird coincidence and doesn't mean a thing, Maryann rationalized. Still, I feel I should share it with Mildred.

Inside, Maryann dialed Mildred's number and waited.

Riders On The Storm

Well, that takes the cake, Troy thought as he watched Maryann drive away. At least she left the cake. He closed the front door, dumbfounded by her abrupt departure.

Alexa played Sonny and Cher, more syrupy pop music. Enough of that tripe, thought Troy. "Alexa, stop music." Storm outside, storm inside, he thought, hearing another loud thunder crack. She clearly didn't buy the story about Julie's insulin vials.

Troy went back to the kitchen to clean up. "Alexa, play 60's Best." Jim Morrison sang about riding on the storm. That's more like it. But why would she care about them? Why would she storm off like that? The look on her face. It was panic and fear. He had seen that look so many times in the service. Troy let out a low groan. Not another loose end. She couldn't know, could she?

Of course not. Gunther confessed. No one would look

any further. Except...those detectives. I don't know Millie, really. That time when *I taught* her how to play pool at the Crow's Feet. She tried to trick me, put me off balance. I should have known better. That conniving bitch knew how to shoot. She's a shrewd one, played on my male ego. It almost worked.

And Ed. I've known him ever since moving into Trivolity. Quiet, unassuming, Colombo-like demeanor. 'Just one more thing', sure. What crap! I know the type. Plays dumb, but notices everything.

Troy paced back and forth through his living room getting more and more agitated.

The two of them working together could be a problem. What do they know? What might they have said to Maryann? I need to find out. Troy put the plates and glasses in the dishwasher. I don't think she bought my explanation, and she seemed to freak out when I went to cut the cake.

Somehow, Alexa picked Queen, the song with 'Thunderbolt and lightning', apropos of the current weather. Oh crap! Her reaction to the knife. The knife! She's afraid of me. That's absurd! I would never hurt her! Bethann gave me no choice. I had to protect the kids. But Maryann, no! She's never done anything to hurt me or my family. It's just bad luck that she saw the vials. I'm sure that

I can explain it away, or better yet, just toss them. There's only four left. I've held on to them for far too long.

He went back to the kitchen and saw the cake still sitting on the island. Troy took the knife and cut a slice, and found a smaller plate for it. Too bad we never had a chance to share it. So nicely decorated all around with almonds. He took a bite. God, that's sweet! Troy almost gagged. It's a good thing I'm not diabetic.

He returned the cake to the saver and opened the refrigerator. Seeing the insulin again, he felt a wave of despair. I need to get rid of them. He looked back at the cake. Margot would be helpless without him. Daniel would continue to f- up. If I'm in jail, then I can't protect her.

It's not really about me. I could go to jail, if it came to it. No one else needs to die. But I need to stay free, my sweet daughter needs my protection. He looked from the insulin to the cake. A sick feeling came over him. He knew what he had to do. Two birds, then.

Troy sliced the rest of the cake, smaller pieces and larger pieces. Women always want the smaller pieces. He retrieved a syringe and latex gloves from the bathroom and reached for the vials in the fridge.

Returning to the kitchen, a lightning flash illuminated the back patio. For a moment, he wondered if someone was out there. Troy went to the door wall and flicked the light on. No one. Satisfied, he turned the light off and went back to the cake.

Carefully, he injected the smaller pieces several times, using up the last of the insulin. He returned the slices to the cake saver.

He quickly searched the Internet for the best way to preserve the pie. Such a handy thing, the Internet. Satisfied with the answer, he put the dessert in the refrigerator.

That's all well and good, he thought. But how do I get her to eat it? She's afraid of me. He went to his office and poured a scotch. The thunderstorm continued, the loud booms urging his thoughts along. Both he and the lightning searched for someone, someone to blame.

Rusty! He was over the other day messing around in the fridge. Might he have touched the vials? Probably. And he has a motive. Or I can come up with one. A lot of people figured out he had a side gig with the pickleball club. I wouldn't be surprised if Bethann had dirt on him. Yes, that could work. Well, old friend, old in Trivolity years, anyway, it's time to throw you under the bus. He took out his phone and texted Maryann as Bob Dylan sang 'It ain't me babe'.

MA, I was shocked and a little hurt when you left so quickly. But then, it occurred to me. You were surprised when you saw the insulin and then I came at you holding a knife; it was a bread knife BTW - you needn't have worried. Was BA killed with insulin? Is that what Millie and Ed are telling you? It wasn't me. What reason would I have? I hate to say it, I think it may have been Rusty. He's always over at my house, mucking around my fridge looking for beer. He would have seen them, too. And I think I may know why he did it. Can I bring the cake back? I can explain it to you then. We may finally nail the guy who killed your sister!

There, that should do it. Troy poured another scotch and contemplated having to kill yet again to protect his family. The things a father must do.

"Alexa, stop music."

Trivolity Justice

Ah, nighttime. Billy Dan drew in a deep breath of fall air, crisp after the sun dropped below the horizon for another day. He idly wondered how many more days and nights he would have to enjoy on the planet; what fate had in store for him. Sighing, he chided himself for being morose. A walk would settle his spirit. He secured the tree house and descended. Others might think twice about wandering the darkened trails, but he'd spent so much time wandering around the property, both as a boy and a man, that each footfall was second nature to him. What seemed odd were all the houses and sidewalks that sprouted where formerly there were only trees.

As he crested the small hill, his ears were met with music thumping from the club. There must be some special event this evening. A dance, perhaps? It wasn't 'prom season', so it couldn't be that. Maybe a Halloween party. He frequently lost track of the calendar, but it seemed like it might be that time of year. Those final days of autumn, when many cultures believed the veil between our world and the spirit world thinned. While others honored their ancestors in various celebrations, Americans had morphed it into rituals that managed to trivialize and sensationalize death at the same time.

Thinking that Maryann wasn't the type to engage in that particular brand of falderal, he decided to cruise by his sister's house. She was more likely to be involved in communing with those in the afterlife in a calm, reflective manner. If she seemed busy, he wouldn't bother her. If she was free, perhaps they could reminisce about Bethann. Poor girl.

As he neared the house, BD was startled to see that nearly every light in the house was burning—at least those on the ground floor. Maryann was more likely to be in favor of low, soothing indirect lighting. He darted between two darkened houses to circle around behind the row of residences. It was something he didn't often do, because people who lived along that stretch backing to the natural areas were likely to have motion detectors installed. Not that they needed them, he smiled to himself.

As he crossed into Bethann's yard, he could see two figures lingering near the kitchen island. From their stances, he could tell their encounter wasn't a happy one. He crept nearer. They were on opposite sides of the island, and a cake server sat between them. Billy Dan knew his sister and Troy had been romantically involved, and though he was no expert, this looked like it might be a lovers' spat. He watched as Troy reached into the cupboard and brought out two plates, followed by forks from the drawer. Maryann was shaking her head. BD inched up close to the house near the sliding door and eased it open just a crack. Their voices floated over to him.

"Troy! I said I didn't want any. Why are you so insistent?"

"Maryann, sweetheart, you worked so hard on this lovely dessert. You deserve to at least take a taste." Troy placed a small piece on a plate, perched the fork beside it, and slid it across the countertop.

Maryann leveled a piercing stare and crossed her arms. "Feel free to have some yourself, but I'm not in the mood for sweets at the moment."

Troy plated a large piece and dug in earnestly, chunking off a large bite and shoving it into his mouth. He didn't wait to swallow before he said, "Thee? Nuffing wong wif ut." He took a moment to get it down his throat. "What has made you so jumpy all of a sudden? This isn't like you." He stepped to his right, around the island. She stepped further right, seeming intent on maintaining distance.

"I...I saw insulin in your fridge, and—"

"I told you! That belonged to Julie; I just haven't gotten around to disposing of it. You just can't flush it or throw it out, and I always miss those 'drug disposal days' at the fire department." He continued to move around the island, as did she. They remained on opposite sides.

"Marynn, honestly. What difference does it make if I have old medication? I'll bet you almost everyone here has a dozen old vials of something or another. I don't get it."

"Troy. Listen to me. Ed and Mil told me that Bethann's cause of death was an insulin overdose."

BD saw Troy's eyes open wide in shock, but it looked like a practiced expression, like he was in a high school theater production, and told to 'look surprised'.

"What? You're kidding me. How awful. Gunther was craftier than I give him credit for."

"And I suspect you know very well that Gunther didn't do it."

Troy brought his hands together in a prayerful gesture. "Maryann. You're not making sense. Maybe you really aren't feeling well. Gunther confessed! People don't confess to murders they didn't commit. Not sane ones, anyway," Troy chuckled, trying yet again to step nearer to

Maryann. "While Gunther is eccentric by many standards, I wouldn't classify him as all-out looney tunes."

BD felt uneasy and debated whether to make himself known. Maryann would be none too pleased with him if she thought he was spying on her. And if he stepped inside now from the backyard, there could be no denying it.

Maryann noticed Troy's aura was swirling red and black. Slowly, she stepped around the island. "Please leave, Troy," she said.

"Why are you behaving like this, darling? We were doing so well, having fun. I can't believe you would toss that all away."

"I'm not throwing us away. I don't feel well. I thought I was better, but it's all coming back. I shouldn't have agreed to see you tonight." Maryann was becoming frantic as she watched the red in his aura take over the black.

"I don't believe you," Troy said. "Something's changed between us. Did those detectives tell you something about me? Huh? Did they?"

"I don't know what you mean!" Maryann said, trying to stay away from him as he circled the island closer.

"Oh, come now. What did they tell you?" he pressed. "I can make you tell me." He lunged for her, but she was quicker, circling to the other side of the island.

"Calm down, Troy. You're scaring me!"

"Scaring you? Why would I be scaring you? Unless you know something that would make you scared?"

Maryann was trembling. She'd lost track of how many times she'd circled the island. It was large, but still. Troy continued his pursuit.

"Why were you paying my sister?" Maryann blurted out. "Was she blackmailing you?"

Troy stopped short. "Oh, so that's it. You found out about the fifty thousand," he snorted. "Well, let me tell you. Your sister was a piece of work. On the one hand, she was a saint. Everyone loved her. But, beneath the smiles lived a snake. She was having sex with anyone who looked at her twice, but just long enough to catch them in her snare. Once she had them, she'd blackmail them for all they were worth. And my worthless son-in-law couldn't keep it in his pants. I couldn't let him do that to my daughter."

"Everyone knows how protective you are of Margot," Maryann said. "Whoever heard of a seventy-five-year-old helicopter parent?"

"Now you're just being cruel," Troy said. "I'm only seventy-three."

Billy Dan took a step back to shake out the cramp in his leg and plowed into a patio chair. "Shit!"

Maryan, startled at the noise, looked toward the door

wall. While she was distracted, Troy lunged around the end of the kitchen island and grabbed hold of her arm. She struggled, but Troy deftly stepped behind her, pinning her to him with an arm across her collarbone. With the other hand, he swept up the small piece of cake he'd plated for her. Holding a palmful of vanilla cake and pudding topped in chocolate, he growled into her ear, "I don't want to do this, believe me, but you figured out how I killed Bethann. This will go easier if you just FLIPPING EAT THE CAKE!"

"It's called Boston Cream PIE," she screamed back at him, and tried to push him away. "You killed my poor sister?!" Horrified, Maryann twisted harder to get free, but Troy was too strong for her.

He mashed the Boston Cream Pie into Maryann's face at the same time BD flung open the sliding door and crashed through the opening, knocking the screen off its runner. Maryann screamed again, and Troy jammed the sticky-sweet mess into her mouth. She spat much of it back out before biting Troy's arm. He howled in pain and pushed her away.

Billy Dan flew across the living room, crouching low. He took down the taller man with a mid-line tackle that sent both men tumbling onto the kitchen floor. Troy thumped his head against a cabinet, which only stopped him for a moment before he began fighting back. BD tried to pin his sister's attacker to the floor, but the former soldier rolled from side to side to throw him off.

"Watch out!" Maryann tried to warn her brother when she saw Troy reaching toward Billy Dan's face, thumbs extended. An ex-army ranger would certainly know how to thumb someone's eyes out and have no qualms about it. BD scrambled away, crawling toward the refrigerator. He tore open a cabinet door where pots and pans were stored. Blindly, he grabbed the first handle he found and swung an eight-inch cast-iron frying pan at Troy. He missed.

"Don't kill him," Maryann shrieked. "Ed, Mil, where are you? Help!"

Both men stopped to look at her. "Who?" they said in unison.

"Either of you. Enough already, just stop!" Maryann was interrupted by energetic banging on the front door. She dashed down the hallway toward the foyer.

"Oh, thank the spirits!" she said as Ed pushed past her, headed deeper into the house. Mil stepped through the sliding door that gaped open, and they arrived together to see the two men crumpled on the kitchen floor, panting.

"I thought I was in better shape," wheezed Troy. Billy Dan gasped for breath in the other corner, still clutching the frying pan.

"We heard the whole thing," said Mil. "Troy Danville, you're under arrest for the murder of Bethann Cook." Ed yanked Troy to his feet as sirens wailed outside the house.

"What the...?" Ed looked toward Mil. She shook her head and shrugged.

"I called 911," Billy Dan said. "I didn't know if I could get inside in time to stop Troy."

"Oh," Ed and Mil said at the same time.

Just then, Deputy Sheriff Barbee, followed by two officers in riot gear, barged through the front door. "What's going on here?" he demanded.

Ed narrowed his eyes as he pushed Troy forward. "I'm arresting Troy Danville for the murder of Bethann Cook. You remember, Officer Barbee, the woman you declared died of natural causes?"

Barbee turned as red as the rose-colored wallpaper he stood before. Mil followed Ed out with a satisfied grin.

The next day, residents of the Trivolity community were all a-buzz. Word spread quickly that something big was happening at the Event Center. Residents came by car, golf cart, and on foot to see what all the excitement was about. It wasn't every day that camera crews from all the local television stations showed up. Questions could be heard murmured through the crowd.

"What's going on?" someone asked.

"It's about the new pickleball court," one resident said.

"That doesn't make sense," said another. "New courts are in the back."

"Yeah," chimed in another. "Why would they set up in front if it's about pickleball?

"It's about the murder," a voice said. "I heard they caught the guy."

"Murder? What murder?"

"What rock have you been sleeping under?" piped another.

Chatter that had taken on a dull roar stopped abruptly when the door to the Event Center opened. Hundreds of eyes followed the Mayor, Deputy Sheriff Barbee, Ed Prescott, and Mildred Maxium as they walked toward the podium. Heads angled for a better view.

Someone whispered loudly, "Hey, isn't that Mil from Step class?"

"That looks like my neighbor, Ed. What's he doing in the middle of all this?" another said.

The response was lost as the mayor stepped forward. He tapped the microphone, which emitted an annoying knocking sound followed by a high-pitched whine. Folks near the speakers covered their ears.

"Oh, sorry! Sorry!" The mayor cleared his throat. "I'm here to announce that we have a suspect in custody we believe to be the perpetrator of the murder of Trivolity resident, Bethann Cook. Thanks go to the coordinated effort of our excellent Sheriff's Department. Now, I'm going to ask the director of the department to step forward to answer any questions you may have."

The mayor stepped away from the podium, his back to Ed and Mildred, who exchanged glances, and gestured for Deputy Sheriff Barbee to come forward. The crowd leaned closer, anxious to hear the name of the murder suspect. Avoiding the intense stares from the real investigators, Deputy Barbee stepped to the microphone and proceeded to thank his team of detectives for their swift work, omitting Ed and Mil, of course. In great detail, he recounted how his department's persistence led to the capture and arrest of Troy Danville.

Mildred leaned towards Ed and whispered, "That bastard!"

The crowd erupted in disbelief at the mention of Troy Danville's name. No one wanted to believe that one of their own could have killed Bethann.

After the sheriff's news conference, Ed drove Mildred, Gina, and Maryann back to his house. It was time to take down the Murder Board. Mildred and Maryann followed Ed into his office. He retrieved three beers from the mini near the desk. "I think we all earned this," he said.

"Even if we weren't acknowledged," Mildred said.

"Hey, I'm used to it," Ed took a draw of his beer. "The grunts do all the work; the politicians take the credit." He smiled and raised his beer to Mildred. "We know what we did. It was a pleasure working with you!"

Mildred raised her bottle, and they clinked them together. "You too, Ed. Besides, we got to know our neighbors a lot better."

"Thank you so much," added Maryann, "Bethann can rest in peace now."

Just then, the doorbell rang, and they heard Gina shout, "I'll get it." Rusty stood outside and smiled when the door opened.

"Hi, Gina, is Ed around?"

"Sure, he's in the office with Mildred and Maryann. Come on in."

Rusty walked into the office and stopped abruptly when he saw the Murder Board propped up in one corner. "What the hell? That's my face with the X over it! And Troy's circled in red!"

"Come on in, Rusty," said Ed, jovially. "Want a beer?"

"Um, sure. Thanks."

"It's called a *Murder Board*," Mildred said. "It helped us to organize our thinking. Sorry, normally we would have this all covered up. But we were just going to take it down."

"Murder Board? You mean I was a suspect? And Kitty, too?"

"Kitty, not so much," Ed said. "I'm glad you stopped by." He took a breath. "Rusty, we need to talk about the pickleball club fees you've been collecting."

Rusty froze. A panicked look crossed his face. He took a deep breath, eased himself stiffly into a nearby chair, his eyes on the floor. His hand shook as he took a large swig of beer. "What are you talking about?" he said.

"A little extra pocket money while collecting dues, eh?" Ed said. Rusty squirmed and almost dropped his beer.

"That's called embezzlement, Rusty," said Mildred.

Defensively, Rusty blurted, "Yeah, well, y'all can't prove nothing!"

"Actually, we can. We have the texts. The texts between you and Bethann, not to mention the rumor mill," said Ed in his best law enforcement voice.

Rusty turned beet red as he reached to set his drink on the desk. It caught the edge, wobbled, and almost tipped over. He lunged to set it right. Sweat was visible on his brow. Clearing his throat, he stammered, "It-it was just a little extra here and there. Those wine dinners are so expensive." He grimaced as if his beer had turned bitter. Mildred looked at Ed.

"What are you going to do?" Rusty clenched his fists and thrust them into his pockets.

"The question is," Ed narrowed his brow and spoke slowly. "What are you going to do?"

"What?" Rusty stared at Ed. "Me?" he said, confused.

"That's what I said. Do I need to repeat myself?"

"No! No! Ahh, I-I mean, I was planning on returning the money. I was-I really was!" Mil snorted from across the room. Rusty turned toward Mil with a pleading expression.

"You know, I should arrest you right this moment." Ed drummed his fingers on his desk. His chair squeaked as he turned his gaze toward Mil. His nod to her was barely perceptible. Rusty began to shake.

Mil got up, brushed past Rusty, and dramatically unpinned his picture from the Murder board. Turning, she said, "Ed and I have a responsibility to report your behavior, and even if we didn't, neither of us condone your actions. Ripping off your neighbors just isn't friendly."

Rusty looked up, his eyes big as saucers.

"Here's what I propose. We'll give you a chance to remedy the situation, but we are going to report you to the Club GM and recommend that you be required to cover everyone's dues for the coming year. It's likely you won't be allowed to participate in any official club in the future."

"And," Ed added, "you will resign from the pickleball club. You and I both know that if word of this got around, it wouldn't be just the money you would have to be worried about. I hear the Paddle Squad is second only to the Mahjong Mafia in gravitas."

Rusty's head nodded vigorously, and he jumped to his feet. "Yes! Yes! Y'all have a deal!" Slowly, he backed toward the office door, then turned to make a hasty retreat.

"Hold on there, Rusty," Mil said. He turned slowly, looking scared.

"We didn't call you here. You came to us. So why'd you stop by?"

"It was nothing, nothing at all."

"Come on!" Ed said. "Out with it. You took the time to get in your car and drive over. It wasn't nothing."

Rusty swallowed hard. "I just wanted to ask you about the news conference. The Sheriff said Troy killed Bethann. But...I thought Gunther did it."

"We did too, initially," Mildred said. "But the evidence pointed to someone else. That's all we can say right now."

Rusty, a dejected look on his face, said, "Troy had a temper. But he hurt no one that I knew of. I have to think that if he did this, he had a damned good reason."

"The evidence is ironclad," said Ed.

Rusty took a deep breath, looking as if he wanted to say something. Instead, he looked around the office one more time, turned, and walked out. A few minutes later, Gina could be heard bidding him farewell at the front door.

"Poor guy," Maryann said.

"Poor guy? He lost my sympathy a long time ago when we learned of his crime against the pickleball club," Mil said.

"I can see what Maryann means," Ed said. "I understand he and Troy were close. Rusty seemed truly shocked that Troy would resort to murder for any reason."

"Troy's a piece of work, but he certainly has a way with people," Mil said. "He duped everyone. You have to admit, Ed, we were both surprised when the evidence called him out."

Maryann stood to leave. "I should get going. I want to thank you both again for what you did the other night."

"No," Ed said. "We have you to thank. If you hadn't played along..."

Maryann paused. "Once I saw the insulin in Troy's fridge, and his attempts to hide it from me, I grew suspicious. After the ME's report, you know."

"Well, you put two and two together."

"I might not have if I hadn't seen Troy's aura go from

bright blue and orange to red and then almost solid black. It was then I knew for sure."

"That Troy killed your sister." Mil gave Maryann a side hug. Maryann smiled weakly and nodded, her eyes filling with tears.

"Still, you took an enormous risk," Ed said, "letting Troy come to your house with your phone connected so we could hear what was going on."

"It was also a good thing that BD was there," Mil added. "Things could have gone badly even though we were waiting outside."

"Go home now, Maryann, and get some well-deserved rest," Ed said as he walked her to the front door.

Mil was already disassembling the Murder Board when Ed returned from seeing Maryann out. "Time to pack all this up," he said, placing a box on the desk and gathering his notes.

Silently, Ed and Mil worked side by side. Through the open office door, a distant phone could be heard ringing. Shortly thereafter, Gina came into the room, phone in hand.

"Ed?" Gina said.

"Yeah, hon."

"You won't believe this! That was the club GM. There's been another murder!"